THE KINGDOM OF WISDOM

THE KINGDOM OF WISDOM

YANK SHI

Contents

Preface

DIVINE WATCH RENEWED

2029 AD

At the end of the book *Interstellar Roaming*, the author mentioned that David and Emily's son Oliver and daughter Sophia, after listening to their parents' interesting stories about their experiences in the star voyage, were determined to follow in their footsteps and embark on a new Interstellar Roaming together. They thought about it day and night, hoping that the opportunity would come and their dreams realized.

Their aspirations moved God.

Each of them had a dream, just like their parents, on the same night. In the dream, God told Oliver that his father's watch had been updated and could be used by Oliver. God gave Sophia a new spell in her dream and instructed her to cooperate closely with her brother Oliver to achieve the predetermined goal and escape from any possible difficult and dangerous situations.

After waking up from their dreams, Oliver and Sophia agreed to experiment to determine whether the artifact obtained in their dreams was effective.

Oliver: You tell me, Sophia, give a goal to move forward.

Sophia: Since the Divine Watch allows us to reach any destination in an instant, regardless of distance. Let's go to Australia. Let's go and see that charming place.

Oliver: Australia is a very large and independent continent. Let's choose the city of Melbourne.

Sophia: Sure.

Oliver: Let me determine the location of this place on the Divine Watch. Sophia, please give the order.

Sophia: Okay.

Sophia silently recited the Magic Spell she had learned in her dream last night.

In an instant, the two of them were in a park in Melbourne, Australia.

Australia's natural environment was different from that of the United States. The flowers, trees, and animals in the wild were also quite unique. They also saw kangaroos and koalas.

The two used their mobile phones to take photos and videos of these fascinating animals and unique environments as a souvenir of their visit.

Later, they returned to Boulder, Colorado, USA in the same way in an instant, almost without any deviation. Oliver and Sophia got up before dawn that day.

They gently pushed open the doors to their grandparents' and parents' bedrooms, gazing at their sleeping loved ones and silently bidding them farewell in their hearts.

They also affectionately stroked the old cat Lily sleeping on the sofa in the living room and said goodbye to her. Lily woke up and looked at them, calling out "Meow" with a glance.

Oliver and Sophia thought that Lily might not know that the two siblings were going on a long journey and would be away from home for many years. However, Lily threw herself into their arms and seemed reluctant to part ways with them.

She didn't know that the brother and sister were going on a long journey and would be away from home for many years.

They left a letter for their parents and grandparents, quite like the one David and Emily left for their family members when they went away and then left home without saying goodbye. Oliver also took away his father's pocket watch with him.

The letter reads:

Dear grandparents and parents,

We love you, every one of you.
Please forgive us for leaving without saying goodbye. Please forgive our recklessness this time.

The Almighty God met us in a dream. The renewed Divine Watch with the Magic Spell has been transferred to us as gifts.

We are grateful for it.

We are willing to complete the sacred mission entrusted to us by God with our modest strength.

We will strive to do a good job in this investigation.

Goodbye, grandparents and parents. We know that the journey is bound to be full of risks. It is also possible that we will never come back again. In that case, we will bid farewell forever to you at this moment. We sincerely thank our grandparents and parents for their upbringing and teaching.

We have the blessing and protection of God and the help of the artifact. We believe

The home of the three generations of Polo was located at the foot of the majestic Rocky Mountains. Oliver and Sophia climbed up the hillside and looked at the lush Boulder City below.

Here, they had serious and meticulous discussions and planned for their upcoming journey. After finalizing their plans, Oliver and Sophia prepared to embark on this extraordinary journey.

Oliver turned on the Divine Watch to select the destination of this trip on the screen.

Sophia: Dad and Mom went to ten planets in a parallel universe. They called that universe Universe B. We can go to a new universe to have a look. We can call it Universe C.

Oliver: OK, I agree.

Sophia: I want to go to a planet inhabited by humans to investigate the lives of people there.

Oliver: I agree. In addition, I am considering choosing a human world with a highly developed civilization. I think human intelligence can be developed without limit, almost endlessly.

Sophia: I fully support your point of view. Let's do it.

Oliver began to search on the screen of the Divine Watch. After multiple comparisons, he finally determined a Wisdom Star with a long human history in the Great Light Galaxy in Universe C. As for the passage of time, Earth's years were no longer a valid measure. In other universes and galaxies, time was not recorded by Earth's standards, which were based on its orbit around the Sun. The Wisdom Star in the Great Light Galaxy of Universe C must have an entirely different reference.

Oliver operated on the Divine Watch and finally confirmed their chosen destination of Wisdom Star in Universe C. Sophia recited the spell. They disappeared from Earth in an instant and arrived at a strange planet in another universe.

Chapter 1

CUSTOMS OF THE WISDOM STATE

The two young siblings, Oliver and Sophia, came to a strange planet called Wisdom Star in the Great Light Galaxy of Universe C. They found everything here remarkably fresh.

This was a place with beautiful mountains. The water in the rivers and lakes was crystal clear. There were large green frogs on the shore. There were fish swimming in the water, and white wild geese foraging on the grass. There were also animals similar to the elks on Earth running about in the wild. The little elks were playing on the grass and chasing each other.

The sunshine here was bright and the temperature pleasant.

However, the sun seen on Wisdom Star was not the same as the sun in our solar system. The sun here appeared slightly larger, but not too hot.

Oliver and Sophia strolled on this unfamiliar land, feeling exceptionally comfortable and refreshed.

As they walked, they heard some melodious music in the distance, which sounded like the sound of a flute and was quite pleasing.

They came to the place where the locals lived, which looked like a village on Earth. However, there were various shops and service facilities, as prosperous and convenient as in a big city.

The houses in the residential area were also different from those on Earth. The design favored graceful curves and circular structures, creating a space perfectly suited for indoor activities and leisure.

The people here were slightly larger than those on Earth. Men, women, children, and the elderly all look very relaxed.

Due to the mild climate and soft sunlight, the skin color of the people was lighter, closer to the white race on Earth.

Oliver and Sophia greeted the people and tried to talk with them. Due to language barriers, they could only roughly guess what each other meant.

Oliver and Sophia found that the spoken language of the people here was quite unique, sounding pleasant, vivid, and expressive. The speech also contained some vowels and consonants that were not present in human languages on Earth.

Oliver and Sophia communicated with the locals mostly with the help of gestures and facial expressions, and gradually reached mutual understanding. In addition, most of the people were warm and friendly, so the siblings didn't feel nervous or awkward at all.

With the enthusiastic help of the locals, Oliver and Sophia were arranged to live in a two-bedroom, one-living-room apartment. The indoor facilities were complete, and this kind of house was considered high-end housing on Earth. Oliver and Sophia were told that the house was free and was a VIP treatment.

Oliver and Sophia asked the locals if they could find suitable jobs for them. They wanted to work. The enthusiastic locals said that they could first go to a school called "Cultural University", to learn the local language, and were exempted from tuition.

So, the siblings began a new life in this novel environment.

They learned that Wisdom Star was a small planet. There was only one country on the planet, called Wisdom State. The territory of Wisdom State covered three large islands and hundreds of small islands on the planet.

They discovered that the people of Wisdom State revered knowledge and talent above all. Those with profound wisdom and versatile skills were chosen as rulers, entrusted with governing the land and shaping the lives of its citizens.

The current head of Wisdom State was Wildum, a highly intelligent scholar and politician.

President Wildum implemented a policy of respecting teachers and valuing education. Therefore, the citizens of Wisdom State generally had a high cultural literacy. Most citizens held college degrees, and those with outstanding academic achievements were given priority for employment in key cultural, political, and business sectors.

All citizens received various types of education and possessed diverse knowledge and skills.

Oliver and Sophia inherited their father and mother's hobbies and liked to talk about Heaven, the stars, and mankind. Sometimes, they discussed and chatted with their classmates. They were surprised to discover that in cosmology and philosophy, the people of Wisdom State shared strikingly similar understandings to those on Earth, with many points of consensus and resonance For example, matter and spirit, the omnipotence of God, the origin of human beings, etc. It could be seen that different planets, even different universes, and the creatures on them were all created and governed by God. People on Earth and people in the Wisdom State were all under the same roof of Heaven.

Most people in the Wisdom State believed in religion.

There were several different religions there, each with its own revered God and deities. Believers of different religions basically lived in harmony, at least without intense conflicts.

There were various rumors about the origins and identities of Oliver and Sophia in the local area. Everyone thought that these two were mysterious aliens—and they were.

Most local people were polite and friendly to these two aliens. Many of their classmates had become their good friends. They enthusiastically help them solve their life and academic problems.

Oliver and Sophia gained a deeper understanding of the shared essence of human nature—humanity itself.

Politically, Oliver and Sophia noticed that the government of this country was very close to the people. President Wildum was very open-minded, placing the interests of the people above everything else and treating himself as a servant of the people.

Oliver and Sophia also learned that this country had police only, but no army, because there was only one country on Wisdom Star, Wisdom State. Since there were no foreign countries, there were no foreign enemies.

Oliver and Sophia believed that this was a democratic country, although people here rarely talked about concepts such as democracy and freedom. They seemed to have been accustomed to this.

Wisdom State fascinated Oliver and Sophia.

Chapter 2

YOUNGER SISTER'S ROMANCE

Time passed swiftly, and before they knew it, Oliver and Sophia had spent nearly three years (by Earth's measure) in the State of Wisdom. They liked the environment, made many friends, and had a comfortable and fulfilling life. They almost felt reluctant to leave.

They had completed their studies at the Culture University and had also found jobs for themselves. Oliver was engaged in software development, while Sophia conducted research on comparative literature. They worked from home most of the time.

By this time, Sophia was estimated to be over twenty years old (Earth era) and had blossomed into a graceful young woman. A mixed-race American and Chinese, she was born in the futuristic world of *The Wonderland*. Her features combined the best traits of both parents, giving her a striking appearance. She was lively, smart, and quite popular.

There was a young man named Huxechin, a recognized handsome man and the dream lover of many girls. He had a graceful manner and extraordinary temperament. Wherever he went, he was always accompanied and courted by girls.

Sophia and Huxechin met by chance at a grand dance party. Huxechin took the initiative to introduce himself and talk to Sophia.

He invited Sophia to dance.

Sophia: I'm not familiar with the dance steps here.

Huxechin: That's okay, I can teach you, it's very simple.

It didn't take Sophia long to get the steps right. The two danced to the beautiful music.

During the dance, Huxechin kept looking at Sophia's face with a gentle gaze. Sophia admired the handsome man in front of her with a deep affectionate look.

As the dance ended, the music lingered in Sophia's ears. Huxechin's face and eyes surfaced in her mind again and again, refusing to fade. In that moment, she realized she was enchanted—her heart had been won.

After the dance, Huxechin invited Sophia to a high-end restaurant for dinner.

The two conversed further over dinner. Huxechin spoke of the upper class in the State of Wisdom, considering himself among its ranks, while Sophia was more interested in the state's cultural origins. He spoke with ease and confidence—though his knowledge was not particularly vast, his charm and eloquence were enough to captivate the girls around him.

Huxechin curiously asked Sophia about the situation on Earth. He was even more fascinated when talking about Sophia's parents traveling through time and space, to the past and future worlds, and to ten planets in another universe.

Since then, Huxechin and Sophia stayed in close contact.

Huxechin had a special affection for Sophia, which inevitably made many people curious. After all, Sophia was an alien from an unknown origin. Huxechin's pursuit of Sophia made other girls somewhat jealous, and they often talked about it behind their backs.

When this matter reached Oliver's ears, he did not support his sister's love affair.

Oliver: Huxechin is very self-righteous, and he looks down on us from the bottom of his heart. I can see this from his behavior and his eyes.

Sophia: I know he's not the same type of person as us. But he loves me, and I love him too, that's enough. Brother, don't you want to make a girlfriend here? There are some nice girls in this state.

Oliver: Don't forget that we are just here to travel and explore. We won't stay here forever. If I get married and have a family here, I won't be able to take my lover away in the future. Our Divine Watch doesn't have this function.

Sophia: Yes, this is a problem. If I can't take my spouse with me, I'll stay here. This is a nice place too.

Oliver: But our artifact must be operated by both of us at the same time, and we can't be separated.

Sophia: So, what should we do?

The romance between Huxechin and Sophia continued to spread.

When Oliver asked about this and still didn't agree with Sophia's relationship with Huxechin, the two argued.

Oliver: I hope you exercise some restraint, Sophia. Getting too deeply involved in this matter will result in significant losses.

Sophia: Brother, I know you're doing it for my own good. But there is a true love between me and Huxechin, and I feel deeply in my mind that there is fate between us. This is arranged by Heaven, and I have no choice.

Oliver: Sophia, you should be more rational. This is not a trivial matter.

Sophia: I know. I am no longer a child.

Oliver: To be honest, I think you should stop here. This is the wisest approach. Wake up a bit.

Sophia: Brother, I hope you won't interfere with my personal affairs. Goodbye.

Sophia turned around and left the room.

For several days in a row, Sophia didn't go home to spend the night. Obviously, she was already living with her lover.

Sophia was completely conquered by love. She didn't care about her future or prospects.

For her, in life, she was with the person she loved the most, nothing else mattered. She felt infinitely happy, which was difficult for ordinary people to understand.

After that, the two often appeared on more social occasions. They sailed the sea on a yacht, soared through the sky in a private plane, and touched down gracefully on a shimmering lake. They swam in the rolling waves, sipped coffee in charming cafés, and toasted with champagne in elegant restaurants. Lost in love, they reveled in the sheer joy of life.

Sophia was glad that she had the opportunity to come to Universe C, the foreign land of Wisdom State. Here, she found her true love. Her heart overflowed with gratitude, endlessly thankful for God's grace upon her. In Sophia's mind, Huxechin was a perfect person, her most admired idol, and her most respected male god.

She believed that her combination with Huxechin was not a coincidence, but a destiny. Sophia liked Huxechin's elegant demeanor, his words, and his deeds. She even liked his sleeping posture and snoring.

Huxechin was a young man who was exceptionally intelligent and talented. He was originally an optimized man created by Professor Pavic. But this was irrelevant to Sophia. She didn't care about this fact. To her, all people in the world were created by God. Huxechin should also be created by God. Professor Pavic just made some optimizations on him.

Once, after Huxechin and Sophia kissed passionately, Sophia gently stroked Huxechin's hair, gazing at him, asking: Dear, are you a real person? Do you have a human soul?

Huxechin asked Sophia nonchalantly: What do you think?

Sophia nodded, stared at her favorite, and answered the question by herself.

Chapter 3

Repaying Resentment with Virtue

ophia was living with Huxechin and the original residence of Oliver and Sophia was now occupied by Oliver alone.

In the Land of Wisdom, people were warm and friendly to Oliver and Sophia and treated them as alien visitors. However, there were some people who were not very nice to them.

When Oliver was in school, there was a young man named Gelza in the class who always liked to pick fights and provoke Oliver. He even gave Oliver an indecent nickname. He called Oliver "Wild Goat". Oliver didn't care at first and took a tolerant attitude towards him.

After graduation, Gelza found a high-end job as a researcher in the Human Optimization Laboratory. He was proud of his high social status and had a sense of superiority. He also held a lofty position as a citizen of a wise country and looked down upon outsiders like Oliver and Sophia.

Gelza had a vulgar personality and took every inch of Oliver seriously, thinking that Oliver was weak and could be bullied.

This Gelza was big and strong, with long hair on his arms and legs, thick black eyebrows, a broad nose, and a big mouth. Oliver looked a little weak in front of him.

One day, Gelza came to Oliver's house to challenge him and shouted and cursed outside the door. He called Oliver a "foreign bastard".

Oliver went out to fight. Without saying a few words, Gelza immediately raised his hand to Oliver.

They wrestled together. The two of them punched and kicked each other, like a boxing match. Since they were not evenly matched in boxing—one a heavyweight, the other a lightweight—Gelza always had the upper hand.

After the fight, Oliver suffered multiple injuries.

Gelza: That's all for today. Mainly to let you taste my fist. I'll come back next time.

Oliver: OK, please come. I will definitely accompany you.

After a few days, Gelza came to challenge again.

Immediately, the two of them hit each other with fists and feet, fighting fiercely.

This time, Oliver found some ways to deal with a strong opponent. He dodged skillfully and made his opponent miss frequently, causing him to fall to the ground several times.

Tension ran high as they grappled, neither willing to back down. Their struggle grew chaotic until they lost their footing, tangled together, and stumbled over the tree roots beneath them. Tumbling down the slope, they crashed onto a gravel field below.

Both were injured—Oliver's back was scraped and bruised, while Gelza, bleeding from a wound on his head, still saw himself as the victor.

The two injured warriors had no choice but to withdraw from the battlefield. They limped away.

Oliver returned to his residence and saw Sophia waiting inside. She had not been home for several days and now came back to visit her brother.

Sophia saw her brother's miserable condition and asked him what happened. Oliver told his sister about the conflict with Gelza.

Sophia was very angry and vowed to teach that boy a lesson.

Oliver: Gelza relies on his big size and big fists to provoke all the time. If you were with us, we could use the Divine Watch to expand our bodies and it would be no problem to overwhelm that guy. But you were not around these days, so I couldn't use the Divine Watch.

Sophia: I'm sorry, brother, I made you suffer. I came back this time to ask for your opinion. I want to marry Huxechin.

Oliver: Let's talk about this later. Now I just want to have a good rest.

However, Gelza's wounds gradually healed, and he was full of confidence. Since he defeated Oliver in a boxing match, he boasted in front of everyone that he easily defeated the aliens and was an invincible general.

He spread the word that he wanted to compete with the big brown bear in the wild. He also set a time for everyone to go to a location in the wilderness to watch and cheer for him.

There were a lot of spectators who came to watch the fight between man and bear that day.

Gelza arrived on time by an automatic car. Oliver and Sophia also went to watch, mixed in the crowd.

After a while, Gelza and the big brown bear appeared at the competition site one after another.

When the whistle sounded, the man and the bear began to fight.

Gelza was tall and mighty in the crowd of people, but he looked thin in front of the big brown bear.

He displayed a power struggle posture, but the big brown bear paid no attention to it, just moving its huge body and swaggering forward.

Gelza clenched his fists and steadied his stance as the massive brown bear extended its powerful paws, baring a maw of razor-sharp teeth.

Yet, Gelza remained composed, unfazed by the beast before him.

At first, man and bear exchanged blows—punches against swipes, fists against claws. But soon, their battle turned into a fierce grapple.

The watching crowd stood frozen, breathless with tension as the fight raged on. Blow after blow, they struggled, their bodies straining until both combatants were left panting, their breaths ragged in the heavy air. Gelza was sweating and gradually exhausted. His endurance was not as good as the big brown bear.

But he still kept shouting to cheer himself up.

Later, his voice became a little hoarse.

The big brown bear became more and more courageous and occasionally roared loudly.

After several rounds of wrestling, it was clear that Gelza was losing. His shirt was torn in several places, tattered from the relentless struggle. He seemed barely able to do more than defend himself, each movement driven by sheer endurance.

He was caught off guard when the brown bear bit him on the back of the neck and held on tightly.

The audience held their breath, their mouths opened, and some even screamed loudly.

Obviously, the scene of human-bear combat was about to result in fatalities.

Due to Gelza's overconfidence in winning this competition, he neither hired a referee nor a paramedic, only one host was responsible for blowing the whistle.

Although there were many spectators, they were powerless.

Seeing this, Oliver and Sophia quickly activated the Divine Watch and they suddenly turned into giants. The two giants strode forward with great strides.

Oliver used his big hands to pry open the brown bear's mouth, Sophia covered Gelza's wound with her hands, carried him away, and called an ambulance with her mobile phone.

The brown bear was somewhat afraid of the sudden appearance of the two giants and awkwardly left the field.

Gelza almost lost his life because of his overconfidence. He received multiple treatments in the hospital before finally recovering.

Afterward, Gelza thanked Oliver and Sophia profusely for saving his life and for repaying evil with kindness, choosing to overlook past grievances.

He was especially humbled when he recalled provoking a fight with Oliver. If Oliver had transformed into a giant to fight back, Gelza knew he would have suffered greatly and been left in utter humiliation. Instead, Oliver had shown restraint, and for that, Gelza was deeply grateful.

This broadened the horizons of the citizens of the State of Wisdom. They looked at Oliver and Sophia differently. People knew that they were divine beings from outer space, with boundless magic power and noble character.

Chapter 4

INTERSTELLAR LOVE

Since the day Oliver and Sophia transformed into giants to rescue Gelza, their heroic act had been the talk of the people. With each retelling, their deeds grew grander, embellished into legend until they became the stuff of myth.

Oliver and Sophia were praised as angels sent by God, bringing happiness and good fortune to the State of Wisdom.

Many beautiful girls in the State of Wisdom fell in love with Oliver and were willing to entrust their lives to him.

Oliver spent a lot of time persuading them that he came to the State of Wisdom just to travel and investigate and that he would return to the distant horizon in the future. Their artifact was exclusively for him and his sister, and could not be shared with others, nor could they bring others with them.

The girls persuaded him and his sister to stay there and not to leave. Oliver said that he and Sophia were destined to go back home to Earth. They would bring the results of their investigation outside to the people on Earth and tell them stories about the outside world. They also need to bring the high-tech achievements here back to Earth.

There was a girl named Miranda who didn't care about Oliver's words of persuasion towards them.

Miranda: It doesn't matter to me whether you stay in the State of Wisdom or leave here in the future. I have entrusted my lifelong destiny to God. I entrust my love to you without reservation.

Oliver: Miranda, you are a good girl, let's just be friends.

Miranda: You have many friends, and you don't lack me, either. What I want is your love and your sincerity. Do you really love me, Oliver?

Oliver looked at this girl with sincere emotions, this exotic girl with a lovely figure and a face like a flower.

Oliver: Good girl, I'm leaving here in a few years. Would you be willing to stay alone after that?

Miranda: Then I'm willing to. As long as we can be together, even if it's only for a short time, I'm willing. Our union should be arranged by Heaven, no matter what our fate may be in the future, I accept it.

Miranda's sincere love conquered Oliver.

They interacted frequently and loved each other more deeply.

Oliver found many advantages in this girl. She was different from ordinary girls. She was gentle and friendly to Oliver, and her feelings were sincere and deep.

Sometimes, Oliver also felt strange that he and Miranda were just casual acquaintances. They were not originally on the same planet, or even in the same universe. Now, by chance, they were together, and they were in harmony and in love. It seemed that both of them thought that their relationship was destined by Heaven.

Oliver noticed that Miranda had an extraordinary temperament and demeanor. Her words and deeds were different from those of ordinary women, exuding a strong sense of sophistication.

Miranda was not rigid. She had her own thoughts and opinions and liked to ponder deeply alone. She liked reading, had a broad perspective, and profound insights. She enjoyed fantasizing, traveling, and exploring.

When she was with Oliver, she especially loved listening to him recount the stories of his parents, David and Emily—their time-traveling adventures and interstellar explorations. Each tale filled her with longing, stirring a deep desire for the day she, too, could journey across the vast expanse of the universe.

When Miranda first learned that Oliver and Sophia—two aliens—had arrived in the Land of Wisdom, curiosity sparked within her. One of her motives was to befriend them, drawn by the mystery of their origins.

Over time, she and Oliver grew close, their bond deepening into love. They understood each other effortlessly, complementing one another in a way that felt almost fated. It could be said they were a perfect match.

They were like-minded and shared the same ideals. They were ambitious and keen on studying the sky, the earth, and people, but they had little interest in politics. Oliver fully understood Miranda's decision to give up her high status as queen and became a commoner, and gave her high praise and appreciation.

Oliver discovered that Miranda had a great musical talent. Miranda enjoyed singing and could also play several instruments similar to the piano, violin, and flute on Earth.

The songs she sang from the Land of Wisdom were very moving and pleasant. Although they were completely different from the music on Earth and sounded purely foreign to Oliver, the music was touching and seemed to penetrate into people's hearts and souls.

Miranda also liked to listen to music on Earth. She asked Oliver to sing for her. He had a beautiful voice and sang beautifully.

Oliver and Miranda sometimes bumped into Huxechin and Sophia in public places.

The two pairs of lovers casually greeted each other and had a brief perfunctory conversation, but it seemed a bit unnatural.

Huxechin appeared somewhat condescending due to his high social status, but Miranda didn't think so. She believed that her previous social status was far higher than Huxechin's. She could have inherited the throne and become the queen of the Kingdom of Wisdom. It was her own choice to become a resident woman nowadays.

As for Oliver and Sophia, they believed that they were the only ones who enjoyed the love of God and had divine artifact in their hands, so they didn't need to be condescending.

Chapter 5

Gifts from the Former King

fter a period of dating, Oliver opened his heart to Miranda, and Miranda also talked to Oliver about everything.

It turned out that Miranda had a distinguished family background. Her father was the king of the Kingdom of Wisdom. At that time, the country belonged to the former Kingdom of Wisdom.

Oliver and Miranda's close friendship was not because Miranda was the daughter of the former king of the Kingdom of Wisdom and a real princess.

Oliver was not an ordinary man. His parents, David and Emily, possessed great wisdom and vision. They were trusted by God with divine artifact. They had traveled through time and space to the ancient and future and had roamed on ten planets in another universe. They had made new discoveries and achievements in cosmology and philosophy.

Under the influence of their parents, Oliver and Miranda were also exploring the universe and humanity.

Whether their union was directed by God, it seemed no joke.

Oliver learned that the previous Kingdom of Wisdom was a good era.

At that time, there was the wise monarch, Molax.

King Molax was diligent in governance and loved the people, valuing education and talent, and managed the country to be prosperous and orderly.

During his reign, although he held the highest authority in the country, he lived a simple life and never indulged in extravagance, let alone pursuing the grandeur and luxury of the court.

In his lifetime, he only had one queen, Queen Monsha. The two had a deep and long-lasting relationship and loved each other for life. After her death due to illness, he truly missed Queen Monsha and did not marry a new queen. Although as a king, he could have many a queen and many concubines, enjoying all the glory and wealth.

King Molax had no sons. When he was old, he intended to let his daughter, Miranda, ascend the throne as queen. But Miranda had no interest in politics.

So, King Molax handed over his power to Wildum, a capable man he trusted.

Wildum was originally the dean of a prestigious university. He was open-minded and advocated political reform in the Kingdom of Wisdom.

His daughter Lankee was a good friend of Miranda. The two often talked, sang, and played the piano together, and had a deep friendship.

Wildum was even more enlightened. Soon after he took the throne, he changed the state system from monarchy to constitutionalism. He was elected as the president of the State of Wisdom. People speak highly of him, calling him *the father of wise democracy and constitutionalism.*

After Wildum took over as the head of Wisdom, he followed the will of the people and governed the country effectively, which made the old king feel very relieved.

The old king knew he was old and his only concern was the fate of his daughter Miranda. The king had always doted on his daughter and regarded her as the apple of his eye.

When the king learned that his daughter was dating Oliver, he approved, acknowledging that Oliver was a good man. However, he knew Oliver could not remain in the Kingdom of Wisdom forever. As for his daughter's future, he chose to leave it to fate, trusting that God would guide events toward their rightful course.

The old king Molax passed away peacefully.

Before the king's death, his daughter Miranda tearfully accompanied and bid farewell to her father who was about to leave.

King Molax asked everyone around him except Miranda to temporarily step aside, saying that he had something important to tell his daughter alone.

The king revealed to his daughter the secrets he had hidden in his heart for many years.

The king said to his daughter: If you don't want to inherit the throne, then forget it, I completely agree with you. In fact, I have long wanted to abdicate and hand over the power of the country to more talented people. Now, Wildum has taken over the power, and I am very satisfied. You are kind-hearted and have no unreasonable expectations. Before I leave, I would like to give you three treasures.

"First, there is a precious book in the palace called the '*Wisdom Encyclopedia*', hidden in the West Pavilion. That is the most detailed essence of wisdom in the Kingdom of Wisdom. The wisdom in it is based on God's instructions. Or it can be regarded as the wisdom of God. I hope you can read this book from time to time, appreciate its mysteries, and benefit greatly from it. When encountering difficult mysteries, answers can be found in this book.

"Second, there is a hot spring on the cliff of the canyon on the East Foothill of the mountain. It is a Sacred Spring. Ordinary birds will become beautiful and their calls will become more melodious after drinking and bathing in the hot spring. People will also become beautiful in appearance and mind after drinking and bathing in the hot spring. However, the hot spring is located on a steep cliff of a deep valley, ordinary people cannot climb up without special skills. This Sacred Spring was presented to the king as a gift by a senior monk, as a way to repay the king's pro-people policies.

"Third, there is a sunken ship in the Great North Sea. On that ship are countless treasures like valuable gold, silver, pearls, and agates."

The king gave his daughter a sea chart with the position of the sunken ship marked on it. If the treasures of the sunken ship can be salvaged, it will be a very considerable income. This sea chart was given to the king by the owner of the sunken ship before his death as a reward for his benevolent governance.

The king said that it would be no easy task to obtain the latter two treasures, and it requires the assistance of some powerful benefactors.

Miranda was deeply grateful for the king's generosity in giving these three treasures.

Chapter 6

SACRED SPRING

Miranda found the wisdom treasure book gifted to her by the king on the West Pavilion of the palace and treasured it. Later, she entrusted someone to input all the contents of this encyclopedia into her computer; with the electronic book and backup, it was more convenient to check at any time.

The other two treasures given by her father were not easy to get. They required significant effort and the assistance of noble people to achieve.

Miranda thought that it would be difficult for her to succeed alone. At this time, she naturally thought of Oliver and Sophia. These two people had magical powers and would definitely help her overcome difficulties and get the treasures.

Not to mention that she had a deep friendship with Oliver. She believed that Oliver and Sophia would definitely help her.

Miranda talked to Oliver about this. Oliver said that he could help to get the two treasures. But to accomplish this, they needed the power of the Divine Watch. And the Divine Watch was jointly controlled by him and Sophia. He agreed to talk to Sophia and let her join their treasure-hunting team.

So, Oliver revealed this to Sophia, and Sophia readily agreed. Oliver urged Sophia to keep the treasure-hunting plan a secret—even from her boyfriend, Huxechin. Sophia assured him of her discretion and solemnly vowed to keep it confidential.

The treasure-hunting team, composed of Miranda, Oliver, and Sophia, discussed together. It was decided to go after the Sacred Spring first.

The hanging Sacred Spring was located on an extremely steep cliff in a deep valley. The cliff was covered with big trees and vines, and helicopters could not approach it.

The treasure-hunting team made a careful plan, brought the necessary tools, and took an automatic car to the vicinity of the East Foothill Canyon.

The three of them entered the canyon and walked through the bottom of the canyon. They cut through thorns and passed through dense bushes.

From time to time, massive pythons slithered out of the bushes, disrupting their path. Fierce reptilian creatures—akin to Earth's crocodiles—emerged as well, their sharp teeth bared, eyes gleaming with menace as they let out eerie, threatening squeals. A chill ran down their spines; their scalps tingled. It was clear—they had stepped into peril. But no one suggested giving up the trip.

At this moment, Sophia suddenly screamed. Her left leg was bitten by an animal and blood was flowing profusely.

Miranda took out iodine from the first aid kit they brought with them, washed Sophia's wound, and bandaged her with a band.

Oliver thought for a while and said: Let's activate the Divine Watch now, enlarge our bodies, and then protect Miranda before continuing to move forward.

Oliver and Sophia operated the Divine Watch, and in an instant, they turned into giants. Sophia picked up Miranda, who appeared small, from the ground and held her in her arms.

Now, the two giants were walking at the bottom of the canyon, and the animals around them turned into mice under their feet. At this time, these mice and small animals looked up and looked at the giants with fear. They were trembling, only worried that they would be trampled to death by the giants.

The treasure-hunting team came to the cliff where the Sacred Spring was located. Oliver and Sophia could easily reach the Sacred Spring on the cliff with their hands.

The Sacred Spring was connected to a large cave. The cave was pitch dark. They peered into the cave just as a swarm of large black bats burst forth, their wings slicing through the air with a sharp, hissing sound.

These bats were unusual. They attacked the newcomers, slamming into Oliver and Sophia's bodies and faces, and making terrible squeaking sounds. Oliver and Sophia fought with them bare-handed, driving away one group and another group came.

Later, bats gradually became scarce and retreated. Oliver and Sophia were bitten several times, still bleeding and in pain.

In the dark corner beside the cave, one could see a huge owl perched there, looking at the two unwelcome visitors with its piercing eagle eyes. Its eyes were shining with a fierce light, enjoying the bats' attack on these unwelcome guests with great interest. It seemed to be the guardian of this Sacred Spring. It could drive away all kinds of birds that fly in to drink water and bathe.

Later, the big owl also stretched its wings and flew away. It was obviously somewhat afraid of the two giants in front of it, and had to give up its responsibility to guard the spring.

Oliver and Sophia used the bottles and buckets they had prepared in advance to get some water from the Sacred Spring and lifted them to the car parked outside the canyon.

Oliver and Sophia used the Divine Watch to shrink their bodies and return to their normal height. After bringing the water from the Sacred Spring home, each of them drank some and poured some of it into the bathtub to take a shower.

After several days, it seemed that the appearance of these three people had undergone some changes. Oliver became more handsome, Sophia and Miranda became more beautiful. More importantly, the hearts of the three individuals had also become more beautiful. They were all grateful to the deceased King Molax.

One day, Oliver and Sophia saw an old woman on the roadside in the wilderness. The old woman was ugly, with a pair of small mouse eyes and an oblique gaze, a hooked nose, thin lips, and half-a-foot-long nails. Her eyes were full of evil. She claimed that she could tell fortunes.

Sophia walked up to strike up a conversation with her.

Sophia: Hello, old mother.

Old Witch: Hello, miss?

Sophia: Can you calculate my future luck for me?

Old witch: You have good luck right now. I can tell from your face.

Sophia: Really? Old Witch: You and your companions have obtained some sacred water. Right?

Sophia: What kind of sacred water?

Old witch: Don't play dumb with me. The black bats have told me.

Oliver and Sophia thought that the black bats in the Sacred Spring Cave were actually accomplices of the old witch.

Sophia: Old mother, what do you think of our future fate?

Old witch: I think it's unlucky. There will be a disaster soon.

Sophia: How to eliminate disasters and solve difficulties, I hope you, old mother, can give me guidance.

Old witch: Come to me again in a few days. I have a magic elixir that can keep you away from evil and misfortune.

Oliver and Sophia: OK, thank you, old mother.

Chapter 7

Underwater Treasures

fter discovering the Sacred Spring, Oliver, Sophia, and Miranda prepared to salvage the underwater shipwreck and obtain the treasure on board.

They knew that this would be a more arduous mission.

The treasure-hunting team first made a careful plan. Oliver found the position of the sunken ship in the sea on the Divine Watch according to the sea chart left by the former king.

They prepared an automatic ship and then the three of them sailed. The sunken ship was far away in the sea, and their ship sailed for a long time, departing in the morning and arriving at its destination in the evening.

Because the sea water was relatively deep, their ship could not drop anchor. They could only let it drift on the sea.

When they discovered the next morning that the ship had drifted far away, they had to realign themselves using the

Divine Watch and navigate back to their previous location.

On the way back, a huge shark chased their ship tightly. Later, there was a storm in the sea, and the big shark took the opportunity to collide with their ship, causing it to capsize unexpectedly. The three people unfortunately fell into the sea.

Oliver and Sophia urgently activated the Divine Watch while swimming, and they immediately turned into giants. The huge shark in the sea was stunned. The delicious food that was about to be in its mouth suddenly became huge creatures that overwhelmed it, so it had no choice but to swim elsewhere.

At this time, Oliver and Sophia's feet touched the bottom of the sea. The two stood in the sea with their upper bodies above the sea surface. To them, the sea at this moment appeared to be just a shallow bay.

Oliver and Sophia escaped safely, but they found that Miranda, who had fallen into the sea, had disappeared. They searched everywhere in the sea, but could not find her. Later, a huge sea turtle surfaced and seemed very friendly to them. It swam back and forth on the sea surface. It kept looking at Oliver and Sophia, as if waving to them and leading them.

Oliver and Sophia gradually understood what it meant, and swam with it. Soon they saw the big shark that had attacked them on the sea surface. The sea turtle swam close to the big shark and bit the shark's jaw. The shark opened its mouth in pain and roared loudly, and Miranda swam out of the shark's belly.

Oliver and Sophia were overjoyed to see this. Miranda escaped death and was out of danger, The two couldn't help but cheer. At this moment, the turtle released its tight grip on the shark's mouth, and the shark fled in embarrassment.

Oliver and Sophia were a little surprised that Miranda was in the shark's belly for such a long time, how could she not be suffocated? Miranda said that she could swim underwater, and there was air in the giant shark's belly, so she survived. Oliver and Sophia said that this was really a miracle and a great blessing.

Oliver and Sophia straightened the ship overturned by the huge waves, and placed Miranda on the ship.

They used their huge bodies to search for the sunken ship on the seabed. Even after searching for a long time, they still could not find it.

The nautical chart they had obtained only provided a rough estimate of the sunken ship's location, marking a relatively large area in the vast sea.

Sophie suddenly exclaimed excitedly, "I've found it!"

She said her feet touched the mast of the sunken ship. Oliver hurried over and found that it was just a bone of a big fish.

After helping Oliver and Sophie rescue Miranda, the sea turtle was still swimming on the sea surface, and it seemed to be leading Oliver. Later, the sea turtle suddenly stopped.

Sure enough, Oliver's feet touched something on the seabed.

Oliver discovered that the sunken ship they were looking for was right there. Oliver exclaimed happily: Found it! Found the sunken ship! Here it is!

Sophia came over. They dragged their ship to a place not far from the wreck.

At this time, the giant Oliver grabbed the wreck from the bottom of the water with one big hand and brought it to the surface. Then the two of them searched the wreck with their hands. As their fingers thickened with their growing size, they resorted to using their little fingers to sift through the wreckage. After careful searching, they finally uncovered several treasure chests.

Oliver knew that he was able to find the wreck at the bottom of the sea thanks to the guidance of the big turtle.

It turned out that the giant turtle had witnessed the shipwreck accident many years ago. On a pitch-dark night, the ship was overturned by violent winds, heavy rain, and towering waves. None of the crew members and cargo on the ship survived. In the years that followed, the giant turtle lingered, waiting for someone to salvage the shipwreck. With a lifespan surpassing that of most marine creatures, it had endured through the ages, surviving to this day.

The giant turtle led Oliver to the shipwreck, and it seemed to have completed its mission.

When Oliver lifted it out of the water and placed it in his big hand to express his gratitude to it, it fell asleep.

It was discovered that the turtle had died. Later, Oliver and Sophia buried the dead giant turtle on the beach by the sea and erected a tombstone for it.

The two took the treasures from the shipwreck one by one to their ship.

They transported these treasures back to Oliver's residence at night. Then they put them in a secret room in the basement.

The treasures inside the boxes were refreshed after a rough wipe. There were gold, silver, gemstones, and agate.

In addition, there was a magnificent crown and a phoenix crown for the king and queen and various jewelry in the box. This was prepared by the owner of the sunken ship, a wealthy businessman, for the king and queen at that time.

The rubies, sapphires, and emeralds here were even more beautiful than similar items on Earth. There were also rare orange, yellow, and purple gemstones unseen on Earth here.

These treasures were all packed in boxes. Although soaked for many years, they were not damaged much.

Miranda counted; there were a total of twelve boxes. Only two boxes had water ingress and partial damage.

Miranda said that these treasures were currently the common property of the three of them. In the future, they would use them to benefit the citizens of the Wisdom Country. This was her father's last wish.

Oliver and Sophia said that these treasures should be owned by Miranda. They didn't have the intention to own them, not even a partial. They knew that they would not be able to bring some items with them when they returned to Earth.

Miranda had another plan. She said that in the future, she could take out a portion of these treasures and use them for mountain excavation for developing the Sacred Spring.

It would be used to build a road in the Eastern Foothill Canyon, leading the road directly to the cliff and Sacred Spring.

Let more people use the divine water of the Sacred Spring and benefit from it. People could become prettier in appearance and more beautiful in spirit through this.

Chapter 8

THE CORNER OF EVIL

The old witch mentioned above was called Qidluss. According to Miranda, Qidluss once worked as a servant in the palace. Due to sowing discord among palace maids and stealing property from the palace, she was dismissed. Because of that, she started harboring resentment towards the royal family and everyone else.

She sought revenge against the royal family and society, scheming in various ways to frame innocent people.

When she learned the secret of the Sacred Spring on the cliff, she decided to occupy the Sacred Spring. She knew that the water of the sacred spring could make people beautiful. Hence, she wanted to prevent people from benefiting from it.

She trained a large owl and a group of large black bats to guard the Sacred Spring, preventing people from touching the water. She wanted everyone in the world to become as ugly and evil as she was.

She was putting in a lot of effort to develop a venom. That venom would enable her to achieve her evil goals.

This poison was a high-end product. It could attack people's spirits. It could make people spiritually corrupt, poisoning people's hearts, brains, blood vessels, and souls.

It could destroy people's spirits and humanity. In other words, it could make people extremely evil. She called this poison the "black heart agent".

Qidluss was cynical and the black poison she had carefully cultivated had great destructive power.

The evil forces of the Wisdom State had begun to rally around her. Unscrupulous individuals flocked to her side, drawn by shared malice—proof that birds of a feather truly do flock together.

Among them was Gelza, the vengeful scoundrel. Harboring a deep grudge against the kind-hearted Oliver and Sophia, he seethed with resentment. Oliver's friendship with the former princess of the Kingdom of Wisdom only fueled his bitterness, and he constantly schemed, waiting for the perfect opportunity to frame him.

The evil forces represented by Qidluss in the State of Wisdom not only poisoned the people, but also targeted the current booming trend of optimized people. They intended to add toxins to the optimized people and make them develop in an evil direction.

Qidluss's evil forces used Gelza to infiltrate the laboratories and production rooms where optimized people were developed and sabotaged. Gelza secretly injected the poison that the old witch had carefully cultivated for many years into some of the optimized people.

Optimized people lack the emotions and morality of real people. Adding evil poisons to them made them even more wicked. The optimized humans, Piruny and Huxechin, were prime examples—both meticulously engineered by Professor Pavic through careful cultivation. After adding venom to their bodies, they turned ruthless and even framed their benefactors and close relatives.

Most villains in the world were not born evil, their malice was generally caused by external factors.

Optimized people had the innate virtues of human beings that were neither good nor evil. After adding venom, one became a complete villain.

In addition, she also developed a large number of flies in the laboratory. She used these flies as small bombers to attack her targets.

The specific method was to breed flies in a large glass box and let them continue to reproduce in the box.

Maggots were crawling around inside the box, emitting a foul odor. She first covered these flies with poison, then released them and let them crawl around the faces and bodies of the victims, infiltrating the poison into people's bodies to achieve the goal of poisoning them.

This ruthless tactic had brought suffering to many innocent people. A person who had been originally kind was filled with evil thoughts after being crawled over by a poisonous fly, and his appearance became ugly, as if he had changed into a different person.

When people learned about the harm of these poisonous flies, they tried to protect themselves and hunt them down.

However, the old witch intensified her evil activities and bred more poisonous flies.

The old witch and the people of the State of Wisdom were in sharp opposition, engaging in a battle of poisoning and anti-poisoning.

Hoards of poisonous flies were attacking people, making it difficult for people to guard against.

The masses battled the swarms of venomous flies using their newly designed fly killers, spraying potent insecticides that wiped out countless pests. The ground was soon littered with the blackened bodies of the dead flies.

But still, things were not working out. Qidluss attacked goodness with evil. Her tricks had repeatedly succeeded. This led to the downfall of the State of Wisdom; the dominance of evil people, and the extinction of good people.

Chapter 9

Repaying Virtue with Resentment

As an optimized person, Gelza was even more proud at this moment. He no longer felt grateful for his lifesavers Oliver and Sophia. He regarded Oliver and Sophia as inferior commoners to him. People considered these two aliens as divine beings. Gelza, however, did not take it seriously. He believed that apart from being able to change and move their bodies with the help of Divine Watch, Oliver and Sophia lacked much wisdom and ability.

However, this Divine Watch was indeed a rare treasure, which made Gelza envious.

Gelza thought to himself—this wouldn't be difficult. A simple trick and the Divine Watch would be in his grasp.

One day, he invited Oliver to dinner at a restaurant. Oliver happened to have some free time and, unaware of Gelza's true intentions, readily agreed to join him.

During the meal, the two of them talked confidently and enthusiastically.

Gelza was very talkative. He talked about the Wisdom Country.

Gelza: The Wisdom Country is a country that thrives on science and technology and is based on wisdom. The country is prosperous and developed, and has surpassed the Earth in Universe A.

Oliver: At present, high technology and artificial intelligence are also being developed on Earth. The Earth is much larger than the Wisdom Planet, with nearly 200 countries.

Gelza: Wow, so many countries. Don't they fight?

Oliver: Sometimes they do. Often because of different ideas, it is difficult for them to always get along well.

Gelza: It seems that Wisdom Planet and Wisdom Country are better.

Gelza asked the waiter to bring two glasses of wine, and when Oliver was not paying attention, Gelza added some hypnotic drugs to his glass.

After a while, Oliver became drowsy and fell asleep on the edge of the chair.

Gelza took the opportunity to find the Divine Watch in Oliver's clothes and put it in his own pocket. He also helped Oliver, who was sleeping soundly, onto the car and escorted him home.

Oliver woke up and found himself lying in his own bed. He was also grateful to Gelza. Later he found that his Divine Watch was missing. He thought that he might have accidentally left the watch in the restaurant after being drunk yesterday.

He called the restaurant to inquire, and the restaurant said that they did not pick up the lost pocket watch.

Only then did Oliver realize that Gelza had picked up the watch. After thinking carefully, he wondered if Gelza had intended to steal his watch.

The more he thought about it, the more suspicious he felt about Gelza.

Oliver called Gelza to ask about the watch, but Gelza never answered the phone.

Oliver was now more certain that the watch must have been stolen by Gelza.

Oliver felt flustered and lost. If the Divine Watch was lost, this matter was not insignificant. Because it concerned the future and destiny of him and his sister.

On the other hand, Gelza was very proud at this time. He thought he had obtained the Divine Watch and he was already a divine being. Gelza tried to activate the Divine Watch. He tried and tried, and finally turned on the watch, with many options displayed on the screen. He selected one of them, but found that the Divine Watch could not start. He issued instructions in the local language, but the Divine Watch showed no response.

Later, the Divine Watch emitted a sound, which was a prompt to guide the use of the Divine Watch.

The prompt said: *Please use the spell to activate the watch.*

Gelza soon realized that the Divine Watch required a spell to function. Without it, the watch was nothing more than a useless trinket in his hands. Frustration washed over him, and he slumped weakly onto the sofa, utterly disheartened.

He was furious and threw the watch into the trash can.

Later, he thought that he might as well return the watch to Oliver to repair his relationship with Oliver.

Gelza picked up the watch from the trash can and went over to Oliver's residence.

Gelza: We were drinking at a restaurant that day, and you got drunk. I found a pocket watch on the ground while helping you onto the car. Do you think this watch belongs to you?

Oliver: It's mine.

Gelza: Take it back.

Gelza handed the watch to Oliver, who took the pocket watch.

Oliver: Thank you.

Oliver knew in his heart about the disappearance of the Divine Watch, Gelza's lics could not deceive him.

He also understood that there were people who repaid kindness with ingratitude.

At the beginning, when Gelza was in danger, Oliver had come to his rescue, saving his life. He never expected gratitude or reward—he only hoped that Gelza would find his conscience, abandon his hostility, and cease his attempts to harm him.

But Gelza remained unchanged. Beneath his façade of kindness, malice still festered. Meanwhile, Oliver, ever trusting, extended his heart to others without guarding himself against those with evil intentions.

Chapter 10

True or False Younger Sister

elza failed to use the Divine Watch, but his thieving intent to seize it did not die.

Through various schemes, Gelza discovered that the activation code of the Divine Watch was in Sophia's possession and that its power could only be unlocked when she and Oliver used it together.

Determined to render the watch useless, he devised a plan to separate them, ensuring they could not activate its magic—effectively stripping the Divine Watch of its power.

Gelza asked Professor Pavic to design and make an optimized Sophia. This optimized person looked very similar to Sophia in appearance, difficult for people to distinguish the real from the fake. Gelza let this optimized person act as a substitute for Sophia, called Sophia SI.

This Sophia SI had collected all the relevant information in advance and was determined to fulfill her mission.

At Gelza's instruction, Sophia SI came to Oliver's residence and talked to Oliver. Oliver thought this was his sister Sophia and had no doubts about her identity.

Sophia SI brought up her relationship with Huxechin again, insisting on pursuing it. Oliver urged her to reconsider, but she remained firm, arguing that Huxechin was a good person and there was no reason to doubt him.

She confronted Oliver multiple times, each conversation escalating into an argument about her marriage. She also strongly defended the optimized people of the State of Wisdom, declaring them a superior race and rejecting any criticism against them.

Sometimes, the two quarreled over these things until their faces turned red and their necks became thick.

Sophia SI sometimes seemed to deliberately provoke Oliver. So, Oliver was really irritated.

He shouted at Sophia SI: Get out of here! Never come to me again!

Once, the real Sophia came to Oliver's residence and was treated coldly by her brother. Sophia patiently explained to her brother about her relationship with Huxechin.

Oliver actually said rudely: Shut up!

The sister was very disappointed and had to leave.

Sophia felt unhappy. She didn't understand why her brother had become so heartless. They were siblings who grew up together and had always had a good relationship.

Sophia hoped that her brother would change his mind and restore their kinship and friendship. Once she went to her brother's residence again, wandering around.

Accidentally, she discovered a girl who looked and dressed exactly like her, arguing with Oliver indoors. Both of them were not calm and full of anger.

Sophia immediately understood that the breakdown of her relationship with her brother was caused by this person.

Sophia broke into the room and asked the girl: Who are you? Why are you dressed like me?

Sophia SI asked back: I am Oliver's sister Sophia. Who are you?

Sophia: You look like me! Are you a stand-in?

Sophia SI: I think you are a stand-in.

Oliver was also very surprised by these two Sophias who looked exactly the same.

He thought for a while and said: How about this, each of you sing a song, and I will listen to your respective voices? I can determine who the real Sophia is by the tone of voice.

The two Sophias each sang a song with a melodious tune and beautiful voice. Oliver could hardly tell them apart.

Oliver: You both sang very well. Now, I will ask you a few questions to see which of you can answer correctly. Then she is my real sister Sophia.

Sophia: Okay, brother, you ask.

Oliver: Our ancestors once had a historical figure. Does anyone of you know who he was?

Sophia: Marco Polo, the Italian explorer of the East.

Oliver: Yes. Who of you knows where your parents traveled to the future world from?

Sophia SI: The Bermuda Triangle.

Oliver: Yes. Who knows which planet our parents first arrived at during their interstellar travel? What animals were there on that planet?

Sophia: Dasor Star, there were dinosaurs on it.

Oliver: Yes. Who knows in which year your parents returned to Earth after their interstellar roaming?

Sophia SI: 2029 AD.

Oliver: Both of you answered correctly. Now I need Sophia to cooperate with me and use the Divine Watch to take the two of us from this room to the square in front, and then come back to the room.

Oliver confirmed the itinerary on the Divine Watch, and Sophia chanted a spell. The two of them disappeared from the room immediately. After they arrived at the square, they returned to the room in the same way.

During this period, Sophia SI disappeared from Oliver's room. Because she didn't know the spell to activate the watch, she couldn't cooperate with Oliver to use the watch. This proved that she was not the real Sophia.

Oliver took Sophia's hand and said: You are my sister, my. Dear sister, I'm sorry, I had a quarrel with you, and I was not calm. Don't be angry with me.

Sophia: Now I think what you said makes sense. I feel that Huxechin and I are not the same kind of people. It is difficult for us to get along completely. He seems to lack genuine human emotions between people.

Oliver: Sophia, you are right.

Chapter 11

The Intelligent Boom

The Wisdom State was a country with highly developed technology and advanced civilization. Its artificial intelligence development level far exceeded that of today's human beings on Earth and also exceeded the "Intelligent World" described in the book *Interstellar Roaming*.

The people of the Wisdom State admired knowledge and wisdom. They believed that knowledge was power and wealth.

During Oliver and Sophia's stay in the Wisdom State, the technology of the country was continuously upgrading. Especially artificial intelligence was advancing rapidly. Various advanced, sophisticated, and cutting-edge theories, technologies, and related enterprises emerged and flourished.

In the Wisdom State, people had been studying artificial intelligence for a long time. Some pioneering scholars of artificial intelligence began to develop "intelligent people". This kind of intelligent people was different from robots. They were generated by gene editing on real people. They managed to eliminate the negative effects caused by gene editing, making these people look like real persons, but their intelligence and abilities were obviously superior to those of ordinary people. The men were tall and handsome, and the women were beautiful and charming.

This kind of intelligent people were later called "optimized people". In contrast, non-intelligent people were called "worldlings".

Professor Pavic, a senior expert in intelligence research, had been developing optimized people for many years. This was his specialty. He was an authority and pioneer in this field.

His proudest work was the optimized man named Huxechin. Huxechin was a handsome and intelligent man.

The bodies of optimized people were selected from ordinary people, called primarches. In fact, most ordinary people were not willing to serve as guinea pigs for optimizers. Only a few people sought to change their current situation through optimization. Primarchs had to undergo complex genetic editing and surgical procedures to complete their transformation into optimized humans. The process inevitably resulted in a large number of failed experiments, producing defective and abnormal individuals. These failures were not retained but destroyed to maintain the quality of the optimizers. In reality, the success rate was low, and most primarchs used as experimental subjects lost their lives.

Near the optimization Laboratory, there was a place where the primarchs were waiting to be optimized. It was a place with a beautiful environment called the optimization camp.

There were more and more primarchs every day waiting to be optimized in the optimization camp.

Professor Pavic was only responsible for the most critical optimization surgery. He didn't even know the final outcome of whether an operation carried out by someone else was successful or not. Only extremely high-quality examples were shown to him.

The handling of defective and scrap products after surgery was carried out by optimization laboratory managers like Gelza and others.

At the same time, artificial intelligence was applied to all aspects of human life and social activities. In particular, optimized people appeared in large numbers, replacing the status of ordinary people in various industries.

Not only public transportation but also shops, banks, hotels, cinemas, performance venues, and other establishments had integrated intelligent human-operated automated services, significantly improving efficiency. Additionally, civil servants, medical personnel, teachers, artists (including singers and painters), actors, bank cashiers, manufacturers, and repair workers had all been replaced by intelligent humans or automated devices.

The university where Oliver and Sophia were studying had also implemented intelligent teaching, which had replaced the traditional professors' lectures.

At first, the students felt uneasy, but after a period of adjustment, they gradually adapted.

The questions raised by students to the intelligent professors could be satisfactorily answered. The consultations between students and intelligent professors, as well as discussions among students, could be conducted in an intelligent manner and were effective.

Oliver and Sophia were somewhat dazzled by the rapid development of intelligent technology on the Wisdom Star.

People were confused about the lack of real service personnel in the service industry and felt uncomfortable with a society without real people.

In addition, they felt that intelligent products could not completely replace human spiritual products.

During a visit to an art exhibition, Oliver and Sophia talked about their impressions of paintings made with intelligent technology.

Sophia: These paintings look quite beautiful and colorful, with a free-flowing and majestic style. But I feel like something is missing here.

Oliver: I think so too. I think such paintings are commodities that can be mass-produced and sold in bulk, as decorations in hotel rooms, or for those lacking artistic taste to buy them and hang on the walls.

Another time, Oliver and Sophia talked about the current literature of the Wisdom State.

Sophia: When I was studying at the university here, I read some classics of the former Wisdom Kingdom. I was surprised to find that some of the literary masterpieces here also feature storylines and character personalities that appear in literary works on Earth. Later I understood that this was the "humanity" shared by all human beings.

Literary works that do not talk about human nature cannot be called literature.

Oliver: I completely agree with you. I have noticed that since the trend of artificial intelligence entered the literary and artistic fields of the Wisdom State, traditional literary and artistic forms have been overwhelmed, and there have been no outstanding literary or artistic works in the Wisdom State, let alone epic and epoch-making heavyweight works.

Sophia: I don't like the large number of intelligent literary and artistic works that are popular now.

Oliver: Although those works have touching storylines and vivid characters, yet overall, they appear to be fleeting, but without wisdom and emotional depth, without expressing human nature, without showcasing the human soul.

Chapter 12

RETROACTIONS

It was estimated that several years had passed since Oliver and Sophia came to the State of Wisdom.

They seemed to have forgotten the Gregorian calendar on Earth. The era here was based on the sun, which was quite different from the era of the solar system in Universe A.

In the Wisdom State, the optimized people had emerged as a new force, and their influence was growing.

During this period, the theory and application of artificial intelligence had made rapid progress in the Wisdom country. Optimized people had extraordinary abilities and superintelligence.

They enjoyed their jobs with ease. The optimized personnel of Wisdom State were pioneers and backbone forces in various fields. They were also conducting new exploratory research, pushing the discipline of intelligence to new heights.

The common people in the State of Wisdom appeared pale in comparison. Their work efficiency was obviously lower than that of the optimized people.

The optimized people would inevitably show a sense of superiority in front of the ordinary people.

In this way, the gap between the optimized people and the ordinary people in the State of Wisdom was getting bigger and bigger. The gap between them was even greater than the relationship between the wealthy and poor classes on Earth.

However, the common people created by God had human emotions, feelings, discernment of good and evil, and clear distinctions of love and hate.

When Huxechin discovered that Oliver and Sophia could transform into giants, he was struck by the realization that there was always a greater power beyond his own—a sky beyond the sky, people beyond people. For the first time, he understood that there were those far superior to him in ways he had never imagined. This awareness humbled him, forcing him to confront the limits of his own abilities, and a quiet sense of disappointment settled within him.

He was not like Gelza, who thought himself superior to the Divine persons and looked down upon Oliver and Sophia.

Especially people believed that Oliver and Sophia were two divine beings created by Heaven. Huxechin wondered, how could the optimized people in the State of Wisdom be compared to the divine beings?

Huxechin believed that although he was carefully created by Professor Pavic, the professor was still a mortal. As a superior-optimized person, he should be superior to mortals in every way and should be able to further optimize himself. Professor Pavic's other optimizer, Piruny, was even more extreme. He advocated overthrowing Professor Pavic and letting optimized people further optimize people. He wanted to establish a Human Optimization Design Institute, to gather the elite among optimized people and engage in the process of further optimizing optimized people.

Huxechin agreed with Piluny's views and ideas and actively participated in the project of the Human Optimization Design Institute.

After several years (Wisdom Era), the optimized population of Wisdom State was increasing, while the worldlings' population was decreasing.

In addition, due to the high work efficiency of the optimized people, they occupied more and more job positions. As a result, a large number of commoners were unemployed and become poor and scum.

Even the original social elites were now in a pitiful situation.

Optimized people had broad intelligence and were almost omnipotent. The optimized people created by the optimized people were more advanced than those created by humans.

Professor Pavic's research results were no longer valued, and the finished products he made were no longer considered masterpieces, ranking among the top. As the highest intellectual elite and authority on artificial intelligence, Professor Pavic's status was now shaking.

The divide between optimized and ordinary people had sparked conflicts and deepened societal divisions. The optimized viewed themselves as superior, discriminating against the common people, excluding them from opportunities, and actively opposing their presence in influential circles. The optimized people were arrogant and unreasonable, mocking the foolishness, clumsiness, and ugliness of the common people. They claimed that the common people of the Wisdom Star should all die out.

The theory of human optimization was rampant in the Wisdom State and the voice of the optimized people replacing the common people was even louder.

That year, the optimizer Piruny led the optimized armed police force to launch a coup, overthrowing President Wildum and dissolving the parliament.

Huxechin served as the commander-in-chief of the armed police force in this coup. He made great contributions to the success of this coup.

During the military operation of the coup, Huxechin led his troops to occupy key departments such as the administration and academia. In fact, it controlled the lifeline of the entire country. They also controlled major media outlets across the country to promote the governing agenda of the new regime to the people of the country.

Piruny was appointed by the Optimizers as the new president of the Wisdom State. In a carefully controlled election, the Optimizers selected their own elite members to form a new Congress, effectively dismantling the previous secular parliament. What was once a democratic and free political system on the Wisdom Star gradually crumbled, giving way to a rigid dictatorship ruled by the Optimizers.

Piruny implemented dictatorship in the Wisdom State and it went smoothly. His ambitions were even more explosive. With the support of hardliners such as Huxechin and Gelza, he directly changed the state system of the Wisdom State to a kingdom, known as the Post Wisdom Kingdom.

Huxechin played a leading role in the reactionary upheaval of the coup and subsequent reforms in the Wisdom Kingdom, becoming Piruny's most trusted accomplice. Branded a traitor, he was destined to be remembered in history with infamy. Under the rule of the optimized humans, the post-coup Wisdom Kingdom defied progress, plunging into political regression, destabilizing the nation, and bringing immense suffering to its people.

Piruny became the king. His followers were transformed into nobles and ministers. Huxechin was appointed prime minister.

People believed that the political transformation from the former Kingdom of Wisdom to a democratic republic was social progress, but the transformation from a democratic republic Wisdom State to a totalitarian Post Wisdom Kingdom was a social regression. Although technological advancements had boosted production efficiency and improved the lives of the upper class, the middle and lower classes suffered greatly from widespread unemployment. Society's culture and ideology began to decline, spiraling into degeneration.

The coup d'état and the oppressive actions of the dictatorship in the Wisdom Kingdom quickly became despised, fueling unrest among the people.

A student protest against dictatorship and tyranny broke out in the universities.

The student leader who led this student movement was Raspic, a student from the Cultural University. He was an alumnus of Oliver and Sophia, and the boyfriend of former President Wildum's daughter, Lankee. Lankee was also one of the leaders of the student movement.

This was a peaceful demonstration and protest, also supported by the citizens.

The wave of demonstrations was getting bigger and bigger, with the potential to break through the court.

The protesting students set up camps in front of the palace, shouting slogans, singing songs, and performing live newspaper plays to satirize the autocratic dynasty.

Oliver, Sophia, and Miranda strongly supported the students' democratic movement. But they did not participate in person considering their special status. Miranda was a princess of the former Kingdom of Wisdom, and Oliver and Sophia were foreigners. Their participation would inevitably give the current regime an excuse to hold the movement responsible. The current dictatorship would inevitably blame the old regime and foreign forces for the turmoil.

Protests and demonstrations spread across the country, and the flames of democracy burned more and more fiercely.

King Piruny was furious and frightened, preparing to flee. He planned to take his family and confidants to a remote island by plane for refuge. With the support of several stubborn aides, he was also preparing to suppress the movement by force.

On the surface, he sent people to negotiate with student representatives, pretending to be submissive, but behind the scenes he was mobilizing a large number of armed police forces and building murderous weapons. He was secretly sharpening his knife and preparing to carry out a large-scale killing spree against the demonstrators.

Raspic came forward to negotiate with the king's minister of state, Qikoko and was close to reaching a peace agreement.

Unexpectedly, one night, a large number of royal armed forces surrounded the demonstrators in chariots and opened fire on the unarmed demonstrators, killing a large number of students and civilians.

This peaceful demonstration was suppressed by a cruel tyrant.

The court was looking for the leaders and core members of this demonstration across the country. Raspic and his girlfriend Lankee were arrested and imprisoned.

After learning about this, Oliver, Sophia, and Miranda discussed how to rescue Raspic and Lankee. At Miranda's suggestion, they once again used the artifact in their hands and asked the Divine Watch for help.

Oliver and Sophia used the Divine Watch to shrink their bodies and entered the cells where Raspic and Lankee were imprisoned. Then they enlarged their bodies and opened the cell door, releasing Raspic and Lankee as well as all the political prisoners imprisoned at the same time.

They first arranged for Raspic and Lankee to hide in their own homes, but later discovered that a swarm of reconnaissance flies released by the old witch Qidluss kept coming to investigate for safety reasons,

Raspic and Lankee were transferred to reliable homes for shelter. When they discovered a swarm of reconnaissance flies approaching, they changed to another hiding place. So, the court never caught the wanted criminals Raspic and Lankee.

Chapter 13

Entering the Tiger's Den

iranda, Oliver, and Sophia gradually understood and became alert to the evil forces of the Post Kingdom of Wisdom. In addition to striving to uphold justice in the Kingdom of Wisdom, they were also investigating the root of evil, exposing the ugly faces and shameless tricks of villains to the public.

Was King Piruny's great evil innate, or was it caused by the designer? This question always reverberated in Miranda, Oliver, and Sophia's minds.

They planned to unravel this mystery and reveal the truth to the world as a warning to future generations.

Miranda thought this was a question worth exploring.

Miranda: I think you two can solve this problem with the help of the Divine Watch.

Oliver: Yes. That's right. We can make good use of our artifact.

Sophia: Got it. We can shrink our bodies very, very small, and infiltrate into the bodies of the evil people. As the saying goes, you can't get the tiger cub without going into the tiger's den.

Oliver: Good idea. We can try to get into the body of the big evil man and investigate the mechanism that causes evil. Sophia and I will take on this mission. Miranda can coordinate and wait for good news outside.

Miranda: Okay, it's settled.

The current king, Piruny, was the chief villain of the Post Wisdom Kingdom. He brought disaster to the country and the people, acted rebelliously, and committed numerous evil deeds. In this way, they determined that the target of this in-depth investigation was King Piruny.

Oliver and Sophia acted according to the plan. Oliver turned on the Divine Watch at night and set the destination as the bedroom of King Piruny in the palace. Sophia used a Magic Spell to issue a command. The two of them came to Piruny's bedroom, where Piruny was sleeping soundly on the bed. The two activated the Divine Watch again and shrunk themselves to a size invisible to the naked eye.

Holding a tiny fluorescent illuminator they made, they dived into Piruny's body through his open mouth.

Oliver and Sophia walked through the interior of Piruny's body, witnessing the human organs and viscera firsthand.

They saw a massive lung rising and falling like a giant bellows, surrounded by a network of arteries and veins of varying sizes, with blood coursing through them in a ceaseless flow.

In addition, there was the digestive system, the interconnected nervous system, the bones that supported the whole body, and the muscles that connected the skeleton and performed different activities.

Each system in the human body performed its duties, so coordinated, so orderly, everything was so rhythmic and energetic.

Oliver and Sophia were deeply impressed by God's ingenious design.

Sophia: The design of the human body is indeed exquisite. However, it makes no difference between good people and bad people.

Oliver: I think so. Human goodness and evil belong to the moral realm. It has no necessary connection with human organ structure.

Sophia: Oliver, look, why is this man's heart black? It should be red, right?

Oliver: That's right. His heart is abnormal, with some scars and potholes on the surface.

Sophia: Wow, and those blood vessels leading to the heart and brain are also black!

Oliver: Look at his brain. It is also black and scarred.

Sophia: In all human anatomy diagrams, the brain is white.

Oliver: Even a pig's brain is white. I understand, this person's heart and brain have been soaked in bad or toxic water, staining them black.

Sophia: No wonder this person is so evil.

Oliver: I understand now. Piruny was not originally a good person, and his body was injected with bad water by villains, so he became a big villain. This bad water is extraordinary. It not only harms people's physiological organs, but also affects people's spirit and morality.

Sophia: This time we infiltrated the evil man's body and found important clues, which is a great harvest.

Oliver and Sophia also took a sample of black water from one of the man's veins and brought it back.

They told Miranda about their experience and exploration of infiltrating the human body. Miranda listened with great interest.

They tested and compared the bad water taken from the evil man's body with the spiritual poison Mind Agent used by the old witch Qidluss, and found that the two were basically the same. In this way, the source of the poison was found.

Miranda, Oliver, and Sophia discussed the good and evil of human beings.

Miranda: I believe that a person's good and evil nature is often shaped by their upbringing.

Sophia: There is a saying in China that '*in the beginning, human nature is inherently good*'.

Oliver: I don't think this statement is quite accurate. It's hard to find an example of being born a little villain or angel.

Miranda: The family environment and social influence on a child's growth are very important.

Sophia: As for optimized people, although they originally lacked human affection, moral sense, sympathy, compassion, warmth, and so on, it is difficult to say that they are inherently evil.

Miranda: However, if the evil liquid merged with a person's already lacking humanity, it would push them further into darkness, turning them into complete demons.

Chapter 14

Opening the Sacred Spring

he people of the Kingdom of Wisdom gradually realized that Oliver and Sophia were not only divine beings from outer space, but also people upholding justice and resisting evil forces. Thus, some righteous civilians in the country began to gather around them.

Their goal was to fight against evil, uphold justice, and benefit the country and the people.

They advocated national unity and opposed the increasingly sharp ethnic confrontation between the optimists and the laity in the Kingdom of Wisdom. They opposed the discrimination and suppression by the optimists against the common people in the Kingdom of Wisdom. They also advocated the welfare of the people.

Miranda, Oliver, and Sophia thought of the Sacred Spring and the treasures that Morax, the king of the former Kingdom of Wisdom, gave to his daughter.

Miranda proposed to take out a portion of the treasure and use it to build a road to the Sacred Spring and link the water from the Sacred Spring at the cliff to the bottom of the canyon so that more citizens could benefit from it. This was also the last wish of the former king.

This project was a private fundraising project that benefited the people. When the project proposal was reported to the royal court, the royal court delayed approval.

The king's confidants raised objections, saying that the project would affect the king's authority and the status of the optimized personnel, and therefore did not support it.

Oliver and his team solicited opinions from the public nationwide, and the project received wide approval and enthusiastic support from the vast majority of the people in the country.

Oliver and his group once again submitted a letter to the court. The court dared not go against public opinion excessively, so it reluctantly agreed, but the court did not contribute any funds to the project.

The members of the Oliver team had made a comprehensive plan for the project and started construction immediately.

They recruited engineers and construction workers.

They used automated bulldozers and various automatic engineering equipment to open a wide road in the canyon of the Eastern Foothills. After completion, all kinds of vehicles could pass through it unimpeded.

On the cliff where the Sacred Spring was located, they built a water pipe from the Sacred Spring to the bottom of the valley. The water from the Sacred Spring could flow directly to the water pipe switch below. People could get spring water by turning on the switch.

The valve and switch for drawing the Sacred Water were located indoors, within a management office built directly over the water pipe. Inside, intelligent Sacred Spring management personnel oversaw its operation. Additionally, a Sacred Spring management agency was established to safeguard and regulate its use and maintenance. They also expelled the owls and bats that once guarded the Sacred Spring under the command of the old witch.

This project benefited many people, especially the common people, they spoke highly of it.

People could optimize themselves with Sacred Spring water without relying on laboratory design and development. So, the optimized class in the upper echelons of the Kingdom of Wisdom was smearing and criticizing the Sacred Spring.

Qidluss was so angry that she jumped to her feet. She spoke out against the Sacred Spring project. She claimed that the Sacred Spring was her private property and was now occupied by a group of desperate criminals. She wanted to let these people go to hell.

Some things truly enraged her. Those she had poisoned with her venomous flies crawled desperately, yet after bathing in the waters of the Sacred Spring, their symptoms vanished. In other words, the holy water had neutralized her poison.

This marked a significant turning point in the battle between the forces of righteousness and evil in the Kingdom of Wisdom.

At this moment, the old witch was racking her brains, looking for some hidden tricks to teach Oliver and his group a harsh lesson.

She knew that the power of the Oliver team mainly relied on the power of the Divine Watch. And the Divine Watch must be operated jointly by Oliver and Sophia. If one of them was destroyed or severely injured, their Divine Watch would become useless.

The old witch wanted to start with Sophia. She knew that Sophia's boyfriend was Huxechin, an upper-class optimized person who was quite favored and loved by the current king, Piruny. It could be said that she was Piruny's confidant.

However, the old witch still wanted to harm Sophia. She was always worried that her poisonous plan would be opposed by Huxechin.

So, the old witch came to the king in this mood to talk about harming Sophia.

The old witch was a person that the current king trusted, for they had similar beliefs. The evil thoughts of Qidluss had been secretly instilled into the king's mind, and this was confirmed by Oliver and Sophia who had infiltrated the king's body for investigation.

The king received Qidluss in the palace. They had a long and secret talk, and finally unanimously decided that Huxechin would try to get rid of Sophia. They were worried that Huxechin would not be willing to do this evil thing that would hurt his lover. If Huxechin refused this mission, they could find another solution for it.

Unexpectedly, when the king instructed Huxechin to carry out this mission, Huxechin agreed readily.

Chapter 15

TREASURE DISTURBANCE

ophia and Huxechin, who were deeply in love, were quite emotionally close. However, over time, their views on some sensitive issues had not always been consistent. Especially in terms of the attitudes towards optimizers and common people, there was a certain divergence between them.

For example, the recently completed initiatives, such as the opening of the Sacred Spring by Oliver and his companions, had been widely welcomed by the people but largely ignored by the court. Huxechin sided with the court, believing that the primary beneficiaries of the Sacred Spring were the commoners of the Wisdom Kingdom. The ordinary people, empowered by the Sacred Spring's water, were undergoing a form of optimization that threatened the privileged status of the optimizers in the kingdom. Therefore, Huxechin sometimes unconsciously showed his disdain for the opening of the Sacred Spring in front of Sophia. Sophia believed that this was a great deed that benefited the country and the people.

Once the two of them talked about this matter at home.

Huxechin: This project costs a huge amount of money. Where did you get this funding?

Sophia: We mainly rely on private fundraising. Since the court does not provide funding, then we will have to rely on ourselves.

Huxechin: Nowadays, due to the widespread application of artificial intelligence in the Wisdom Kingdom, a large number of people who originally worked in the manufacturing and service industries have lost their jobs. Most of them were unable to contribute. The people were all poor commoners. Where did they get the money?

Sophia: We are not all commoners.

Huxechin: Yes, you still have two divine beings, including you, do you have any money?

Sophia: Don't worry, we naturally have a solution.

Huxechin: I don't believe it. What can the poor do?

His words hurt Sophia's self-esteem.

Sophia: We are not all poor. We have a treasure trove, and we can't run out of funds.

Huxechin: You have a treasure trove?

Sophia suddenly realized that she had just let it slip.

Sophia: I was just joking with you. Forget it.

The shrewd Huxechin kept this in mind.

Huxechin reported the matter to the court. The court also believed that the matter was very serious and should be further investigated.

Huxechin also found the old witch Qidluss and talked to her about this matter. The old witch had long harbored resentment towards those who took her Sacred Spring.

The witch was very concerned. She agreed to investigate the matter. She wanted to focus on Miranda, Oliver, and Sophia.

Sophia now lived with Huxechin, and the treasure trove could not be with her.

Oliver and Miranda lived together and were the key suspects.

The old witch used all her tricks and sent out her bats and flies to hover around Oliver's house all day.

Once, Miranda happened to go to the basement to get something, and some bats and flies took the opportunity to fly in. They found some boxes and sea moss on the surface of the boxes and hurried back to report to the old witch.

The old witch immediately realized the mystery. She thought that these boxes were very likely the treasures that Sophia said, salvaged from the bottom of the sea. Obviously, Oliver's basement was the treasure trove that Sophia referred to.

The old witch excitedly reported her significant discovery to Huxechin.

Huxechin immediately dispatched armed police to surround Oliver's residence and conduct a search of the basement. Sure enough, eleven boxes containing treasures were found in the basement. The police stuck seals on the basement doors of Oliver and Miranda's house to prevent people from entering it. Then the police withdrew, claiming that they would send a cash truck tomorrow to retrieve the boxes.

Oliver, Sophia, Miranda, and their team gathered together to discuss countermeasures. They must never let the treasure fall into the hands of the police and the court. Those treasures were gifted to Princess Miranda by the former king, and they were painstakingly salvaged from the sea.

Oliver and Sophia activated the Divine Watch and found a deserted island on the sea, which they called Treasure Island. There was a cave on Treasure Island where treasures could be hidden.

That night, they moved the treasure boxes out of the basement, loaded them onto an automatic car, and drove to the seaside under the cover of darkness, where they had prepared an automatic ship beforehand. They carried the boxes containing treasures onto the ship and sailed it to their destination at sea. Because the voyage was long, it took them a long time to reach Treasure Island.

After arriving at the Treasure Island, they moved the treasure box by box into the cave. The cave was located in a very secluded place in the valley, surrounded by weeds and shrubs.

After the work was done, the people returned by ship.

The next day, when the police drove a money truck to Oliver's house to collect the treasures, they found that the seal of the basement had been torn off and the treasures in the basement had disappeared. The police sternly questioned Oliver and Miranda where the boxes had gone. Oliver said he didn't know it.

The police: You have committed a serious crime by tearing off the seal and taking away the property without authorization.

Miranda: Those treasures were given to me by the former king and are my personal property. You have no right to take them away.

The police said that they would report the case to the court and punish the people involved.

Oliver and Miranda were accused of hiding and stealing the royal treasure, and they were warned that they could be prosecuted and convicted at any time.

Chapter 16

ELIMINATING THE EVILDOER

s mentioned earlier, the old witch Qidluss once worked as a servant in the palace of the former Kingdom of Wisdom. Having been dismissed for wrongful conduct and misdeeds, she was harboring resentment towards the former royal family and everyone else.

The king of the former Kingdom of Wisdom had passed away, and the king's only daughter Miranda was still alive and in love with the alien Oliver, living a comfortable life.

The old witch felt very uncomfortable about this and thought that the best way to retaliate against the former king's chamber was to attack Miranda. Harming and killing Miranda was the only way to relieve her deep hatred.

In this way, the old witch racked her brains to try to make a highly toxic poison. She would use this poison to harm Miranda and everyone she hated. She extracted venom from poisonous snakes, scorpions, and other venoms, and then concentrated and strengthened it. She created a highly toxic poison and named it "Death Liquid". It was different from the "Mind Agent" Qidluss developed to distort people's minds. The old witch applied the Death Liquid to mice, rabbits, and sheep, and these poor animals died immediately. Later, she applied it to the face of a big brown bear, and the brown bear's face became full of holes, its eyes were blind, and its entire face was ugly.

This poison could harm the bodies of people and animals, which was different from poisons that harm people's spirits.

The old witch was proud and wanted to do something to Miranda.

She closely followed Miranda's whereabouts. Finally, she found an opportunity.

That morning, Miranda went for a walk by the lake alone, breathing in fresh air and quietly listening to birds chirping.

Qidluss, who was hiding in the nearby bushes, suddenly jumped out and poured the deadly liquid from the bottle onto Miranda's face. Miranda's face was covered in venom and she felt severe pain. She touched her face with her hands, and her hands were also in pain after being stained with venom.

Miranda screamed loudly, and pedestrians on the road came to see what had happened.

Oliver also ran out of his house upon hearing the bad news.

At this time, the murderous old witch took the opportunity to slip away.

Oliver helped Miranda back home and rinsed her face and hands with water. Oliver called an ambulance and took Miranda to the hospital for treatment.

After preliminary examination and emergency treatment by doctors, Miranda was no longer in danger of death.

Miranda suffered multiple injuries on her face and was blind in one eye. A few days later, Oliver accompanied Miranda out of the hospital.

During this period, Sophia and several friends came to see Miranda every day, taking good care of her and comforting her.

Oliver began to track down the old witch, the murderer of this case.

The murderer used such brutal means to harm the innocent Miranda. Everyone was filled with righteous indignation and determined to punish the murderer and uphold justice.

Although Qidluss did many evil things and harmed the common people of Post Wisdom Kingdom, she was highly appreciated by the court and was appointed as the Privy Councilor of the Post Wisdom Kingdom's think tank.

But Oliver was also determined to avenge Miranda. Oliver and Sophia had been looking for the old witch.

Finally, they found the demon Qidluss hidden in the thick bushes.

They dragged her out and put her in the daylight.

Oliver: Qidluss, why did you harm Miranda?

Qidluss: This has nothing to do with you.

Sophia: Miranda is my relative, how can you say it has nothing to do with us?

Qidluss: Did you know that her family once persecuted me?

Oliver: You did evil first, you deserve it.

Qidluss: Then Miranda deserves to suffer a bit.

Oliver: Shut up. Your death time is coming.

Oliver took out the Divine Watch and set the option for both of them to grow larger, while Sophia recited a spell.

In an instant, the siblings turned into giants. Qidluss looked up at the two giants in front of her, and she couldn't help trembling.

Oliver lifted his foot and kicked the old witch to the ground.

The old witch was like a little mouse under the feet of an elephant.

Sophia: Step on her, step on this old witch!

Oliver exerted force under his feet, and the old witch screamed in pain.

She kept shouting: Spare me, spare me. I will change my ways and never do evil again.

Oliver: Qidluss, you have committed heinous crimes. Your poison has killed countless innocent people and created countless villains. It has caused the Wisdom Kingdom to be like this today. Can I believe you when you say you want to change your ways?

Qidluss: I swear to Heaven, if I break my promise, I will be struck by thunderbolts.

Oliver pressed down with increasing force, and from the old witch's wounds, a thick black liquid seeped out, a clear sign of the evil coursing through her. Yet, upon closer inspection, a thin strand of blood-red fluid clung to the edges of the darkness— its hue unmistakably human.

Oliver couldn't help but feel pity for the weak in his heart. He let go, sparing the life of the evil woman.

The old witch was extremely grateful to Oliver. And she said she would spend the rest of her life doing good deeds to atone for her sins. She told Oliver to wash Miranda's face with water from the Sacred Spring every day and her facial injuries would heal.

Miranda's face had shown some improvement after receiving several treatments at the hospital.

Later, they used the water from the Sacred Spring multiple times to wash her face, and surprisingly, her face almost returned to its original appearance. Her blind eye also gradually healed and even remained intact as before.

The old witch was half paralyzed and sat in a wheelchair all day, she was still alive. People heard that she really changed her evil ways. She drank Sacred Spring water every day and bathed in it. The black blood in her body gradually turns red.

She refused to continue cooperating with the court, persecuting the common people. She no longer bred poisonous flies or prepared poisonous agents. She also advised people to do good deeds, accumulate virtue, and be tolerant of others.

If this was indeed the case, it meant that even if there was still a little bit of humanity left in the wicked, it would make her repent and start with a clean slate.

Chapter 17

SPARING NONE

A2
TESSA

As mentioned earlier, the Post Wisdom Kingdom had completed its transition from a democratic society to a totalitarian society under the promotion of radical optimization. The authoritarian king of the Post Wisdom Kingdom, Piruny, implemented a series of policies across the country that went against public opinion and in a reversive direction.

They destroyed traditional culture, desecrated moral ethics, and eradicated humanity.

Under the rule of King Piruny, this country was carrying out a plan to exterminate the common people. He believed that only by eliminating all the laity could the optimizers fully exert their efficient role.

The extremists who optimized people actively participated in this devastating action.

The new regime of the Post Wisdom Kingdom implemented a black terror like the Cultural Revolution on Earth and a Nazi-style massacre throughout the country.

The whole country was in chaos, and the police were arresting people everywhere. They first locked people up in concentration camps, and a large number of common people became prisoners and lambs to be slaughtered.

Later, the new regime of the optimized people clearly announced a death order for the common people of the Post Wisdom Kingdom. The Police Department issued drugs to every common person, ordering them to be euthanized.

The bodies were loaded onto a dump ship and taken to the distant sea. As the ship drifted over the water, schools of large fish swarmed beneath it, drawn by the scent of death. One by one, they lunged at the corpses, tearing into the flesh with relentless hunger. Many met their final rest not in graves, but in the bellies of the deep.

Ordinary people who were unwilling to take medicine to commit suicide would be transported by helicopters to some deserted islands far away in the sea, where they would fend for themselves. There were only some wild grass and shrubs on those deserted islands, no fruits, no potatoes. There was no fresh water necessary for human survival. Some people occasionally picked up some clams and the like on the seashore, but it was difficult to fill their stomachs. In addition, there were often strong winds and rainstorms on the deserted islands, and the living conditions were extremely poor. Almost no one who was sent to the deserted islands survived.

Although there was only one country on the planet of Wisdom, and there were no hostile countries, nor wars between two countries, or world wars between multiple countries like on Earth, the massacres within the Kingdom of Wisdom were no less brutal than the wars between countries on Earth.

Oliver and Sophia saw many of their fellow villagers, classmates, and colleagues die in this massacre. They deeply experienced the ruthlessness and cruelty of the dictatorial king and court, as well as the optimized people.

Oliver and Sophia gritted their teeth and were heartbroken.

Miranda burst into tears. She saw that the once beautiful Kingdom of Wisdom had become what it was today.

Oliver, Sophia, and Miranda were wandering in the wilderness. They talked about the current great slaughter in the Kingdom of Wisdom.

Miranda: I don't understand why humans kill their own kind.

Oliver: Often it arises from conflicts of interest.

Sophia: It's always difficult to avoid conflicts between people due to differences in opinions and demands. This kind of conflict is commonplace on Earth.

They accidentally discovered a rabbit's nest in the grass under a hill, where there were four lively and cute rabbits inside. Sophia picked some tender grass nearby and handed it to the little rabbit to eat. The little rabbit ate grass and was not afraid of people.

Miranda: Animals don't have the same worries as humans.

Sophia: I really want to be an animal, free from worries.

Oliver: But animals also have natural enemies.

Sophia: That's still better than the human world.

Miranda: I want to be a bird, flying freely in the sky.

Oliver: Let us entrust our next lives to the cycle of creation, returning as animals shaped by nature's design.

Miranda: Okay, it's settled.

Chapter 18

DEATH OF HEROES

LANKEE
RASPIC

The people of the Kingdom of Wisdom were all worried about the current situation. People generally felt that all hope for survival had been severed by the cruelty of the rulers and the massacre of civilians, pushing them beyond the limits of endurance.

Some dissenters, unwilling to accept the status quo, began secretly discussing ways to resist. Peaceful protests—marches, demonstrations—had been met with brutal suppression, as the dictators had no intention of making concessions. It was clear that this approach was no longer viable.

In the end, the only option was to resort to force. Due to the authoritarian regime's control over the entire state machinery, and a powerful modern armed police force armed to the teeth, fighting against them was like hitting the stone with an egg.

Dissidents in the Kingdom of Wisdom, such as student movement leaders Raspic and Lankee, as well as Oliver, Sophia, Miranda, and others, gathered together to discuss ways to resist tyranny.

Raspic proposed a motion to behead the leaders of the Kingdom of Wisdom, declaring that their tyranny had gone too far and could only be ended through decisive action. The primary goal is to eliminate King Piruny and Prime Minister Hakusechin. Who would carry out this task? Everyone thought that Oliver and Sophia were the most capable. They could use their Divine Watch to get close to the target and then take decisive action. But Sophia felt embarrassed. She said that she couldn't do anything to Huxechin at the moment, after all, he was her lover. In addition, everyone also considered that Oliver and Sophia were outsiders after all, and it seemed improper for them to carry out this task.

Raspic and Lankee volunteered to shoulder this sacred mission. In this way, it was decided that Raspic and Lankee would be the assassins of the king and the prime minister, with Oliver and Sophia assisting them in making all necessary preparations.

Due to the strict security monitoring and alarm system around the royal family, it was difficult for ordinary people to approach the palace and the king's residence. Oliver and Sophia could use their magic watches to cut off these systems on the night of the action so that Raspic and Lankee could act according to the plan. Miranda was more familiar with the structure and paths of the palace, and she could help draw up a roadmap for the mission.

They were ready and chose a date. That night, Oliver and Sophia had already cut off the palace's security monitoring and alarm systems, and Raspic and Lankee sneaked into the palace according to Miranda's route map. Everything went smoothly. Just as the two were typing in the entry code on the keyboard in front of the king's bedroom, a huge owl suddenly swooped down, fiercely colliding and scratching on the keyboard. This caused a password error and triggered an emergency alarm. This alarm was not included in the palace's monitoring and alarm system.

Realizing that the action had failed, Raspic and Lankee prepared to flee.

Huxechin, who lived nearby, heard the alarm on the keyboard of the king's bedroom and immediately led several armed police officers to patrol the courtyard. They met Raspic and Lankee on a narrow path by chance and arrested them without saying a word.

Oliver, Sophia, and Miranda were deeply saddened to learn that Raspic and Lankee's brave actions had ended in failure.

Raspic and Lankee were imprisoned in a mysterious prison. No one knew the location of the prison.

They were convicted of treason by the authoritarian monarchy of the Kingdom of Wisdom without trial, for attempting to kill the king was the top sin in the Kingdom of Wisdom.

Their crimes were widely spread in the media, calling them traitors and demons.

They were sentenced to death by electrocution.

The video of the execution was repeatedly played in the media, warning people that this was the inevitable outcome of resistance.

Oliver, Sophia, and Miranda paid tribute to the two brave warriors who sacrificed their lives for the country's and people's freedom. They were infinitely sad about their departure.

They also felt sorrow for the suffering citizens of the Kingdom of Wisdom.

All three of them unconsciously shed tears.

When they learned that the chaos caused by the owl had directly led to the failure of their operation—and that this very owl had once guarded the Sacred Spring for the old witch Qidluss—they decided it must be punished.

Miranda said that she had an eagle called Viter that could help her get rid of the evil. Miranda asked Viter to find the evil owl and give it a taste of pain.

Miranda's eagle Viter really lived up to everyone's expectations. He went out to search for the evil owl and collected the debt that killed their two heroes.

A few days later, the eagle returned triumphantly and brought back a pair of eyes of the evil bird owl.

The same is true in the human world. Those who serve evil masters as evil slaves often end up worse off than the evil masters themselves.

Chapter 19

STONES FROM OTHER MOUNTAINS

liver was worried about the current situation in the Kingdom of Wisdom. What puzzled him was whether the progress of human technology would inevitably lead to the extinction of mankind itself? Could the future of the Kingdom of Wisdom represent the fate of mankind on all planets?

Oliver looked for the answer in the Book of Wisdom again with a question.

When he asked the book this question, the book gave the following answer: The progress of human technology should benefit mankind, not destroy it.

The pessimistic future of the Kingdom of Wisdom did not represent the fate of humanity on all planets.

The current dire situation in the Kingdom of Wisdom was caused by the improper operation and handling of some individuals on the planet.

The optimized human designed and made by humans went against God's will and was not real persons, but a kind of counterfeit. The governance and development of a country led by such individuals would inevitably lead to the country's demise.

The Book of Wisdom suggested that Oliver and Sophia use the Divine Watch to take a look at another planet in the Great Light Galaxy of Universe C, "The Bright Wisdom Star". The situation there was completely different from that of Wisdom Star.

Oliver felt as if he had heard the voice of God. A ray of light suddenly shone into his confused heart. He discussed this with Sophia and Miranda. Everyone felt the same way. The three of them agreed that Oliver and Sophia would personally go to Bright Wisdom Star with the help of their Divine Watch to observe and investigate the specific situation there.

In this way, Oliver and Sophia took the lead and determined the itinerary to Bright Wisdom Star without hesitation. Oliver found the coordinates of Bright Wisdom Star on the Divine Watch, and Sophia recited the spell and issued the signal.

The two arrived at Bright Wisdom Star in an instant.

Bright Wisdom Star was also a small planet. The natural conditions were similar to those on Wisdom Star.

The landing site of Oliver and Sophia on Bright Wisdom Star was located within the territory of Bright Wisdom country. There were still three small countries on the planet.

This country was in a stage of highly civilized development. Oliver and Sophia first toured the country, finding it remarkably orderly and well-organized. Everywhere they went, human activities exuded a sense of ease and harmony, creating a relaxed and pleasant atmosphere—so unlike the tense, oppressive environment of Wisdom Star.

They had settled down in Bright Wisdom country and planned to spend a few days to thoroughly examine everything here.

They were the first to experience the local customs in Bright Wisdom Country, witnessing the lives of people from all walks of life, the relationships between society and family members, and so on. Ordinary People lived happily and harmoniously, filled with the kind of familial bonds and sweetness in life that the Wisdom nation gradually lost and deeply longed for.

In fact, the level of technological development in Bright Wisdom Country was no less than that of the Kingdom of Wisdom, and artificial intelligence and automation even surpassed the Kingdom of Wisdom in many aspects. Robots were exquisitely designed and widely used.

What surprised Oliver and Sophia the most was that Bright Wisdom Country did not have the majority of optimized people in this country. So, there was no ethnic confrontation between optimized people and ordinary people.

Oliver and Sophia began to understand that a highly developed civilization and society could achieve social progress without relying on artificially optimized people.

Wald, the governor of Bright Wisdom country, warmly received the envoys from the Kingdom of Wisdom. Oliver and Sophia expressed their desire to understand the national conditions of Bright Wisdom Kingdom and learn from its experience in governance.

Governor Wald was somewhat like Wildum, the former president of Wisdom State, reasonable and approachable.

When it came to governing the country, he said that the principle he valued the most was people-oriented. All progress and development of a country should be for the well-being of its citizens. He expressed great concern upon learning about the current situation in the Post Wisdom Kingdom. He knew that the Kingdom of Wisdom had once had a wise king and the Wisdom State had an enlightened president. Unexpectedly, technological progress had turned a once prosperous country into a living hell.

Oliver and Sophia highly agreed with Governor Wald's governance philosophy and policy for the Bright Wisdom country.

The two saw a completely different national destiny and future in another country. They understood that the Kingdom of Wisdom could have developed in another direction and avoided the current disasters.

Oliver and Sophia returned to the Kingdom of Wisdom with new knowledge and ideas. They talked to Miranda and other like-minded people about their trip to the Bright Wisdom Country and what they saw and learned there.

Everyone felt the same way. They became more aware of the absurdity of the politics of the current Kingdom of Wisdom and the hopelessness of its future.

At the same time, they also agreed that Miranda should come forward to give advice to the current king, because Miranda was a citizen of the country, and it would be inappropriate for outsiders Oliver and Sophia to come forward. They hoped the king to learn from the practices of the Bright Wisdom Country, change course, and get the country back on to the right track.

Miranda mentioned an idiom that Sophia often said in her talks, "A stone from another mountain can be used to attack jade."

It meant that one could learn from the experience of others to solve one's own problems.

Miranda's advice was flatly rejected by the king, who declared that he would severely punish dissidents such as Miranda, Oliver, and Sophia, accusing them of misleading people and spreading false rumors.

Miranda: Since the king is so heartless, why don't we fight against him?

Sophia: We can use our artifact to eradicate the cruel and tyrannical king and his forces, and liberate the enslaved people.

Oliver: The matter is not that simple and requires careful consideration. Nowadays, the optimizers have an absolute advantage in the Kingdom of Wisdom, and they possess weapons of mass destruction. If they use these weapons when we attack them, not only will we fail to win but more innocent people will suffer.

Sophia: Yes, although we can become giants, we have no weapons.

Oliver: Of course, we can also manufacture weapons. Considering the civilians in the concentration camp and the large number of individuals in the optimization camp, they are all innocent civilians. We can only try our best to avoid armed conflict.

Chapter 20

The End of
the Wisdom Star

uxechin was the Prime Minister of the Kingdom of Wisdom, who also oversaw the police department and had full authority to mobilize the armed forces. This person was ruthless, like the head of the Nazi Gestapo back then. He directly deployed and controlled the extermination of the secular people.

Huxechin had the idea of getting rid of Oliver and Sophia. These two extraterrestrial humans possessed superhuman abilities. If they were allowed to stay, there would be great troubles in the future. Besides, there was already an order to get rid of Sophia. He could definitely take advantage of this opportunity to eliminate the secular people and kill them. This was really a godsend opportunity.

He had a plan to exterminate the common people in batches. The list included all the names of the secular people who were confirmed to be exterminated.

Sophia found herself on this list as well. She couldn't believe it was true, her eyes were blurred and she almost fainted. The lover she once loved so much was so heartless that he didn't even spare her.

Sophia met Huxechin and asked about this. Huxechin actually confirmed it as if nothing had happened.

Huxechin: You are a vulgar person, and I can't do anything about it. I can't disobey the orders from above. We must go our separate ways. Goodbye, my former love.

Sophia: You are a heartless and ungrateful thing!

Sophia left in anger. She was extremely disappointed. She found that she had fallen in love with a ruthless and cold-blooded person. Only then did Sophia realize that Huxechin's love for her was just a show. The handsome man Huxechin who once made her love deeply was actually a hypocrite. Later on, Sophia discovered that Huxechin had leaked information about their treasure to the court, and began to have a gap and be wary of him.

Huxechin originally had several girlfriends, who were all optimizers. Since he met Sophia, he found that Sophia's feelings for him were sincere and deep. He resolutely got rid of his previous girlfriends and dated Sophia alone. Now his official career was at its peak and his political status had greatly enhanced. He also felt that it was beneath his status to have a secular girlfriend, and he was thus under a lot of pressure in the upper class, so he harbored the thought of breaking up the relationship with Sophia.

When Professor Pavic learned that he was also included in the list of purged secular, he couldn't believe it and thought it must be a careless mistake.

Professor Pavic came to the palace alone and tried to figure out the matter, asking King Piruny for an explanation. He was stopped by the palace guards. After multiple negotiations, he was finally allowed to enter the palace.

King Piruny warmly welcomed his benefactor Professor Pavic in the palace.

Professor Pavic mentioned that he was included in the list of people to be eliminated. King Piruny said it was simply a careless error.

He asked his subordinates to remove the professor's name from the list immediately.

Talking about the current situation in the Kingdom of Wisdom, Professor Pavic expressed his dissatisfaction. He hoped that the king could change his political goals and current policies.

King Piruny said that he could understand. The country was currently in a critical period of social change and transformation, and the current chaos would inevitably lead to great order in the future.

Professor Pavic said that he hoped to leave here and go to a peaceful place.

King Piruny said no problem. He also said that he would send an unmanned aircraft to take Professor Pavic and his family members to an island called Anle Island, where the scenery was beautiful and the climate pleasant. The residents on the island lived a well-fed life.

Professor Pavic agreed to this arrangement.

Sophia learned about this from Gelza. Gelza also said that this time Professor Pavic's family would never come back.

When Oliver heard this, he frowned and said: That's too bad.

The professor's family is probably in trouble. Although Professor Pavic created some evil optimized people, that was not Professor Pavic's original intention.

Sophia: We have to find a way to save Professor Pavic's family.

Miranda: I think there may be something wrong with the unmanned aircraft that King Piruny sent to Professor Pavic.

Oliver and his companions found an aircraft expert named Kimraff and they arrived near Professor Pavic's residence with him, where they saw a plane already parked.

Kimraff inspected the plane and said that it had no landing mechanism and was a "death plane". Everyone understood now. Unexpectedly, they all sighed: The king is so cruel!

Oliver, Sophia, and Miranda found Professor Pavic and explained the matter to him. Professor Pavic was also shocked and puzzled by King Piruny's ruthlessness.

Oliver and the other three were trying to find a way to get the professor's family out of danger.

They thought of Bright Wisdom Country on Bright Wisdom Star, where Oliver and Sophia had been. That would be the best place for the professor's family.

Sophia: But going to another planet requires the help of a Divine Watch.

Oliver: Professor doesn't have a Divine Watch, is there any other way?

Miranda: The Wisdom Country has very advanced spacecrafts. Can we find a way to get the professor and his family to Bright Wisdom Star by a spacecraft?

Oliver and the other two discussed countermeasures with Kimraff.

Kimraff said that the Wisdom Kingdom had several standby spacecrafts. One of them could take the professor and his family to any planet in the Great Light System. He could be the pilot of the spacecraft. He also had a desire to leave Wisdom Star long ago. It was just that he didn't have the exact coordinates of Bright Wisdom Star.

Oliver found the accurate coordinates of Bright Wisdom Star for him on the Divine Watch.

So, Professor Pavic and his family, along with Wildum, the former president, and Kimraff himself, boarded the spacecraft piloted by Kimraff and flew to the Bright Wisdom Star.

It was said that Professor Pavic was highly honored and appreciated by Bright Wisdom State. He was given full play to his talent in developing optimized people there, especially leading human optimization in the right direction to avoid the emergence of bad optimized people.

However, according to the information sent by aircraft expert Kimraff from Bright Wisdom Star, Professor Pavic himself later suffered from serious depression. He always said that he committed serious sins in the Kingdom of Wisdom, created some evil people, and caused great disasters in the Kingdom of Wisdom, and he was in extreme pain and committed suicide.

Miranda, Oliver, and Sophia in the Kingdom of Wisdom had all received death notices from the court. If they did not take the medicine for euthanasia, they would be exiled to a deserted island in the open sea.

Oliver and Sophia searched for information on the Divine Watch and discovered that Wisdom Star, located in the Great Light Galaxy of Universe C, was on the brink of destruction. This revelation reminded them of their parents, David and Emily, who had once used the Divine Watch to foresee the impending catastrophe on their home planet, Dasor. Just as their parents had bid farewell to the native dinosaurs before escaping, Oliver and Sophia now faced a similar fate, wondering if history was destined to repeat itself.

Oliver and Sophia decided to escape from the Wisdom star. It was no problem for the two of them to escape, but what about Miranda? They remembered that their parents said that they took a little dinosaur with them when they escaped from Dasor. They could also give it a try this time, and it would be best if they could take Miranda with them.

Oliver, Sophia, and Miranda would use the Divine Watch to escape from Wisdom Star and return to Earth after a long absence, to their home in Boulder, Colorado, USA, and to their parents David and Emily. It would be great if Miranda could go with them.

Oliver confirmed the destination on the Divine Watch, Sophia chanted a spell, and the three hugged each other tightly. They left Wisdom Star without knowing it, Oliver and Sophia were pleasantly surprised to find that Miranda was with them. The three of them landed in Boulder on Earth at the same time. It turned out that God gave Miranda extra help to accompany them.

The Wisdom Kingdom was now in a state of desolation.

God saw the situation on Wisdom Star and remained calm. He said that the star's end was coming. He flicked his finger, and the Star of Wisdom vanished into thin air. The king and subjects of the Kingdom of Wisdom, those proud optimizers, and the few remaining poor mortals had perished without a trace.

This group naturally included King Piruny, Prime Minister Huxechin, and key court officials such as Gelza. The old witch Qidluss, seated in her wheelchair, was also among them, along with a vast number of primarchs loyal to the optimization camp. Additionally, there was the Sacred Spring, which had long served as a blessing to the people, and the vast hoard of gold and silver treasures hidden on Treasure Island.

All of them vanished in an instant. This was exactly the end of the world that parents David and Emily witnessed back then.

Postscript

RETURNING HOME

With the help of the Divine Watch, Oliver, Sophia, and Miranda left the impending destruction of the Wisdom Star and the Kingdom of Wisdom on it, and in an instant arrived at their original home in Boulder, Colorado, USA, returning to their parents David and Emily, as well as their elderly grandparents.

David and Emily were overjoyed to see their son, daughter, and a beautiful girl from the Kingdom of Wisdom after many years.

Sophia: This is Miranda, the former princess of the Kingdom of Wisdom. She is Oliver's lover, and Oliver is about to marry her.

Parents David and Emily greeted Miranda happily. Their eyes and tone were full of joy and love.

Oliver and Sophia's grandpa and grandma, who were now over 80 years old, were so happy that they couldn't stop smiling.

David: Wow, our Oliver brought back a beautiful princess from outer space. Thank God for the gift.

Emily: Miranda, do you like it here? Miranda: I like it very much. First of all, I saw the affection of my family, the warmth of my home. This made me feel nice and gratified. Mom and Dad, are there any optimized people here?

Emily: What are optimized people? We have never heard of it.

Sophia: Optimized people are a race created by the Kingdom of Wisdom with artificial intelligence. These kinds of people are beautiful in appearance and intelligent, but they are excessively arrogant and look down on ordinary people. And they exterminated ordinary people. If we don't leave there on time, we will be exterminated.

David: This is terrible. Artificial intelligence should benefit mankind, but when it is taken to the extreme, it destroys mankind itself. In the eight years since you left, artificial intelligence on Earth has made great progress. It has been applied effectively in some fields.

Oliver: We have been away from Earth for eight years! We thought it was only five or six years.

Emily: Don't you see that your father and I are much older than when you left?

David: We are both over 50 years old now.

Sophia: But you don't look that old, and you are still quite energetic. Has anything changed in the family over these years?

Emily: Our cat Lily passed away. She was buried in our backyard.

Sophia: I want to go see her. I love her so much.

Everyone followed Sophia to the backyard. Seeing that the once-alive Lily was now buried under a pile of brown earth, Sophia's eyes became wet and some tears flowed unconsciously.

Oliver: If there was no help from the Divine Watch, the two of us and Miranda would have been buried on the Wisdom Star, just like Lily is now.

Miranda: The Wisdom Star has vanished after we left it. We will have no place to be buried if we stay there.

Oliver: That's right. Thank God for returning us to Earth and life.

Before this trip, Oliver and Sophia had heard their parents tell interesting stories about the things they had experienced during their six years of interstellar roaming. The brother and sister were fascinated. That's why the two of them set out on an adventure to travel to the planet of wisdom. Now the situation was reversed. Parents David and Emily were interested in the experiences and stories of their children Oliver and Sophia on the planet of Wisdom and asked them to tell them one by one. These stories had also been told for about one thousand and one nights.

When Oliver and Sophia mentioned the Sacred Spring on the cliffs of the Wisdom Planet, David and Emily remarked, "When you first came home, we noticed that you both seemed more radiant than before. So, it turns out the water of the Sacred Spring was the reason."

www.ingramcontent.com/pod-product-compliance
Lightning Source LLC
Chambersburg PA
CBHW041047310726
48978CB00011BA/453